W9-BJJ-294

Logan sighed, his heart crushed by the weight of his promise

The promise he hadn't fulfilled. He couldn't keep putting it off.... Throwing back his head, he closed his eyes and wrote his mental checklist of attributes essential in a suitable bride.

LOOKS: plain, but not distractingly so
HEIGHT: average
BUILD: neatly assembled, but unobtrusively so
MANNER: modest
ATTITUDE: nonargumentative

He drew a line under "nonargumentative."

Sara Wynter—now *there* was an argumentative female. In fact, the woman he was looking for was the very opposite of Ms. Sara Wynter....

Grace Green was born in Scotland and is a former teacher. In 1967 she and her marine-engineer husband, John, emigrated to Canada where they raised their four children. Empty-nesters now, they are happily settled in West Vancouver in a house overlooking the ocean. Grace enjoys walking the sea wall, gardening, getting together with other writers…and watching her characters come to life, because she knows that, once they do, they will take over and write her stories for her.

Grace Green has written for the Presents™ series, but now concentrates on Harlequin Romance®…bringing you deeply emotional stories with vibrant characters.

Books by Grace Green

HARLEQUIN PRESENTS®
1323—TENDER BETRAYAL
1475—RISK OF THE HEART
1539—WINTER DESTINY

Don't miss any of our special offers. Write to us at the following address for information on our newest releases.

Harlequin Reader Service
U.S.: 3010 Walden Ave., P.O. Box 1325, Buffalo, NY 14269
Canadian: P.O. Box 609, Fort Erie, Ont. L2A 5X3

The Wedding Promise
Grace Green

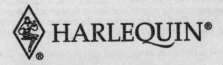

HARLEQUIN®

TORONTO • NEW YORK • LONDON
AMSTERDAM • PARIS • SYDNEY • HAMBURG
STOCKHOLM • ATHENS • TOKYO • MILAN • MADRID
PRAGUE • WARSAW • BUDAPEST • AUCKLAND

If you purchased this book without a cover you should be aware
that this book is stolen property. It was reported as "unsold and
destroyed" to the publisher, and neither the author nor the
publisher has received any payment for this "stripped book."

For Moyra Tarling, Kay Gregory and Kathy Garner
because they've been there from the beginning

And for Barbara Schenck
because of Taggart!

ISBN 0-373-03526-8

THE WEDDING PROMISE

First North American Publication 1998.

Copyright © 1998 by Grace Green.

All rights reserved. Except for use in any review, the reproduction or
utilization of this work in whole or in part in any form by any electronic,
mechanical or other means, now known or hereafter invented, including
xerography, photocopying and recording, or in any information storage
or retrieval system, is forbidden without the written permission of the
publisher, Harlequin Enterprises Limited, 225 Duncan Mill Road,
Don Mills, Ontario, Canada M3B 3K9.

All characters in this book have no existence outside the imagination of
the author and have no relation whatsoever to anyone bearing the same
name or names. They are not even distantly inspired by any individual
known or unknown to the author, and all incidents are pure invention.

This edition published by arrangement with Harlequin Books S.A.

® and TM are trademarks of the publisher. Trademarks indicated with
® are registered in the United States Patent and Trademark Office, the
Canadian Trade Marks Office and in other countries.

Printed in U.S.A.

CHAPTER ONE

THE woman at the wheel of the cabin cruiser was a blonde.

A drop-dead-*gorgeous* blonde, Logan noted as he glowered at her through the brass telescope set up in the bay window of his sitting room. She had the face of an angel and an eye-popping figure set off by a flirty yellow dress—but though he could appreciate beauty as well as the next man all he felt now was irritation.

Intense irritation!

He'd come to his island summer place for a purpose and the last thing he wanted was uninvited company. But this craft so gaily riding the choppy waves of the Juan de Fuca Straits was headed *directly* for his waterfront property.

He swung the scope to the boat's name: *Zach's Fancy*.

Muttering under his breath, he swung the powerful instrument up again...

In time to see someone join the woman at the wheel.

A man, dressed in black, with the dark, rakish looks of a pirate and a physique to match. He smiled and draped an arm around the shoulders of his female fancy...who was, Logan recognised with distaste, young enough to be his—

A bell rang somewhere in Logan's head and he frowned.

Refocusing the scope, he brought the man's face in so close that the silver strands in his black hair were visible.

5

Good God. Logan blinked. Zach Grant!

Movie idol, modern-day Valentino, swinging bachelor. A tabloid wouldn't have been a tabloid without a lurid spread on Hollywood's most notorious womaniser and his current sex object.

What was the name of that rag Andrea was forever poring over? *SuperGossip*? *GossipIsUs*? Whatever: Grant's mug had adorned it only last week. Andy had pointed it out.

'Look, Dad, he's with Felicia Mosscov, that new red-haired model! She's hot…and isn't *he* something?'

'He's something, all right,' he'd muttered, before telling his daughter to put the magazine in the trash where it belonged. She hadn't, of course.

It was at times like those that he realised just how much Andy needed a mother.

Soon, he mused grimly, she would have one.

He jerked his attention back to the boat, and saw that the small craft had now almost reached his dock.

Tension snapped at him like a yappy dog. He shoved the scope aside and stormed across the living room, and the foyer, and then out of the open front door.

Damned intruders! He leaped down the flight of narrow steps, charged down the sloping lawn and thundered across the narrow strip of sandy beach to the jetty.

The sign at the end of the dock was executed in electric blue lettering and its message was clear:

'PRIVATE: KEEP OUT.'

These idiots should have been able to see it by now. They should have been changing direction, and heading back out into the Strait. They were not. They were pulling in alongside the jetty. Logan saw red.

'Ahoy there!' He pounded along the wooden boards.

The couple turned to look up at him.

The breeze caught the woman's glistening blonde hair, blowing it across her face. When she swept back the pale strands, he saw that her eyes were an unusual turquoise colour, and as they met his her expression of vulnerability took him by surprise…and touched something deep inside him that hadn't been touched in five years.

Memories of Bethany, memories he'd managed to hold at bay ever since he'd returned to the island just hours ago, suddenly flooded his heart till he could hardly bear the pain. As a result, when he spoke again, his voice had a cold harshness that was quite unwarranted.

'You can't tie up here.' He fisted his hands on his hips and glowered at the intruders. 'This is a private jetty.'

Sara's first glimpse of the man looming down from above threatened to buckle her knees. For a second, she'd thought it was Travis. Like her ex-husband, the stranger was tall and superbly built, dark-haired and attractive. But even as dismay curdled through her she realised the resemblance was superficial. Travis's hair was brown; this man's was black. Travis's face was pale; this man's was tanned. Travis's eyes were tawny; the stranger's were green.

Green and cold and hostile. And when they skimmed from Zach to her she detected a flicker of contempt.

Her hackles rose, and she felt Zach's arm tighten around her shoulders, deliberately, warningly.

'This is Madronna Island?' he asked.

'That's right.'

'And this is the Logan Hunter estate?' Zach raised his brows.

'Right again.' The stranger rammed his hands into the

pockets of his grey cotton shorts. Despite his casual attire every line of his body, from the arrogant set of his head to the confident set of his wide shoulders, indicated authority. 'I'm Hunter, and this is my private property.'

'The house.' Zach nodded towards the enormous white house situated up on the crest of the hill. 'You live there, I assume. But the cottage—'

Sara, for the first time, noticed the cottage. It was huddled beside a stand of trees, the setting sun pinking the white-painted stucco walls and glancing off the window-panes.

'Yeah, the cottage?' The man sounded as if he was having a struggle to control his temper. 'What about it?'

'I've rented it for the next couple of weeks. Till the middle of July.' Zach withdrew a neatly folded form from the breast pocket of his black T-shirt. 'Through—' he glanced at the form '—Hunter West Realty in Vancouver.'

'No way! Not this cottage, you haven't—'

'Yes.' Sara finally found her voice. 'We have. Zach, tie up the boat and let's get settled in.'

'Right, love.' Zach scooped up the line and started to secure the vessel.

Sara put a hand on his shoulder to steady herself, and stepped off the deck onto the jetty.

She could feel the stranger's hostility coming at her in almost palpable waves.

'Excuse me,' she said, lifting her chin haughtily and making to go past him.

He moved to stand in her way.

Resentment formed tight bands around her skull. *'Do you mind?'*

He didn't budge. 'There's been a mistake.' His tone brooked no argument. 'The cottage is not for rent.'

Zach heaved a large red cooler, a box of groceries and a travel bag onto the jetty. He bounded after them, and the wooden structure shuddered under the impact of his weight.

'If there's been a mistake,' he said firmly, 'it's not mine. OK, you obviously didn't want the place rented out, but somebody in your office screwed up. You *are* the owner of Hunter West Realty?' He held out the contract.

After a tense moment, the other man took it. He scanned it. His lips tightened. He thrust back the form.

'Somebody's head's going to roll,' he snapped. 'But in the meantime I'll fax my Vancouver office; we'll find you somewhere else—and since the mistake was ours it'll be a five-star chalet, and I'll absorb the difference in price—'

'Here we are—' Zach tucked the contract back into his pocket '—and here we stay. You're going to have to make the best of it.' He swung up the cooler and travel bag. 'Sara, can you manage the groceries? Good, then let's get going. Sun's well over the yardarm—time for us to have a drink.'

Logan Hunter stood his ground. 'I'm putting this property up for sale. I need to have ready access to the cottage, to show prospective customers around.'

'No problem.' Zach took off along the jetty, with Sara at a half-run to keep up with him. She could hear Hunter; he was right behind her. 'Sara, love, have you the key?'

Sara slipped it from the deep pocket of her dress as they crossed the beach. When she and Zach reached the cottage, she had the key ready. She unlocked the door quickly and stepped inside, with Zach at her heels.

'Wait!' Hunter's voice had a distinctly frustrated edge. 'We need to talk.'

'You know what they say,' Zach called back over his shoulder. 'Possession is nine tenths of the law.'

He slammed the door shut, and ushered Sara through to the shabby living room. Dropping the bag on the worn beige carpet, he looked at her with twinkling blue eyes.

'The man thinks you're one of my floozies.' He slapped his hand solidly against his thigh as he chuckled. 'Does that bother you?'

'Of course not!' Sara kept her tone light, made it slightly scornful. The last thing she wanted was for Zach to guess how off-balance Logan Hunter had made her feel. 'I don't give a toot what he thinks of me. He's the most hateful man I've ever met!'

Her lips twisted cynically. No, not the most hateful. Travis occupied that position. But certainly the second most hateful. And what rotten luck that Zach should have happened to choose this particular cottage for her holiday. He and her mother had wanted to give her a break, now that her divorce from Travis had finally come through. A time alone, a time for healing, a time for her to regain some peace of mind.

Peace of mind? With Logan Hunter sending hostile vibes her way from his rambling two-storey house on the hill?

Fat chance!

'Daddy.' Andrea Logan skidded to a halt just inside the kitchen doorway. 'There's somebody down there on our beach!'

Logan tightened his grip on the handle of the vegetable knife, sliced the blade viciously through the hothouse tomato on the cutting board, and turned to his daughter.

'Yeah, I—' He stared disbelievingly. 'What the *hell* have you done to your hair?'

She put a hand up to the cropped brown strands that now raggedly cupped her head, dropped it again. And shrugged.

'Cut it.'

But the careless twist of her thin shoulders was belied by the unmistakable welling of tears in her huge brown eyes. Tears she blinked back, but not before Logan had seen them.

She padded in her bare feet to the sink, and stood looking out, her back to her father.

Logan put down the knife, closed his eyes, suppressed an oath.

You've done it again, Hunter, he jeered silently: opened your big mouth and jammed both size eleven feet right in it.

Being the father of a motherless thirteen-year-old, he was fast discovering, wasn't any cakewalk. Andy had been so easy to bring up...until she'd hit her teens. Then—wham! Overnight change, from angel to—

'It's Zach Grant!' Andrea whirled round, her eyes no longer shining with tears, but with excitement. 'Daddy, the man on the beach, it's—'

'Zach Grant. I know.'

'But what's he doing here? Did you invite him? Why didn't you tell me? I didn't know you knew him. When did he arrive?'

'He's here because somebody in one of my offices screwed up,' he muttered. At least Grant was good for one thing—taking Andy's mind off his reaction to her new hairstyle. 'I did *not* invite him—I have never *met* the man before. They arrived when you were burning up the phone talking to your friend Chrissie in Vancouver; he's rented the cottage for two weeks—'

'And the lady with him—'

Logan snorted. Lady! That was a joke.

'—she must be his latest girlfriend. Ooh,' she squealed, 'he must've dumped Felicia Mosscov already. Wait till I tell Chrissie!' She swivelled back to the window again and all but climbed up onto the sink, to get a better view. 'But this one—she looks *way* cool, Daddy!' She turned again, and this time her eyes were veiled, but behind the veil there was a spark that set off a warning bell in Logan's head. 'I think I'll go for a walk.' She made for the door.

Logan snaked out an arm and caught her by the tail of her shirt. 'Young lady,' he said, 'you will do no such thing. I don't want you talking to these people. The man's got no morals, and as for the woman—'

'I don't plan to talk to them,' Andy said smoothly. 'I won't.' She grimaced. 'Do you think I'd want Zach Grant to see me with my hair like this?' She leaned up and kissed her father on the jaw. 'OK, the cut was a mistake, but when we go back to Vancouver I'll get it styled properly. Pax?'

Pax. It was what Bethany had always said when they'd had one of their teasing arguments and she'd wanted her own way. Andy knew it, had always known it, and played it like an expert. He had no defence against it. Against the memories.

'Pax.' He managed a grin as he ruffled the dark curly disaster. 'But get back here in half an hour and we'll eat. How was Chrissie, by the way?'

Andy called back over her shoulder, 'Fine; she and her folks are coming by this way one day next week— they're going to spend a couple of nights at their cabin on Galiano and Chrissie's allowed to invite me along. Can I go? I told her yes, I knew it'd be fine.'

She was gone before he could answer, and his 'Yeah, that'll be OK' bounced back at him from the kitchen walls.

'Zach...'

'Mmm?'

Sara looked up at him uncertainly. 'I have the oddest feeling somebody's watching us.'

Zach took her hand and swung it as they walked along the beach, just below a stand of trees. 'Somebody is,' he said. 'We're being followed.'

'Why didn't you say something?'

'It's just a teenager. I spotted the kid up there in the trees, a few minutes ago. Probably holidaying in one of the properties further along. I believe there are four or five other houses on the island.' Zach yawned. 'Let's go back now, honey. I'm going to hit the sack early. I was up at five today, and I need to be out of here again at the crack of dawn tomorrow.'

'Sure. Boy or girl?'

'Boy or girl what?'

'The teenager.'

'Oh. Girl. Punky haircut.'

'Where exactly did you see her?'

Zach looked round, scanned the treed area. 'Over there...but she's gone. Not nervous, are you?'

'Good heavens, no. I haven't a nervous bone in my body.'

'That's what I thought...otherwise I'd have rented you a de luxe condo where you'd have crowds of people around.'

Sara shuddered. 'I've had my fill of de luxe, Zach.

And I like to have my own space. Need it right now, actually…so the cottage is great. No frills. Back to basics. Just perfect. I really do appreciate you and Mom setting this up for me. Ever since I found out about Travis and—' her throat tightened and she couldn't get the words out '—you know…I somehow haven't been able to get myself together enough to organise myself out of a paper bag!'

'We've both been worried about you. But now that that rotter's finally *legally* out of your life you can start to put the pieces together again.'

They'd reached the cottage door. Zach opened it, and stood back to let Sara pass.

She glanced around again, just before she went inside, and that was when she saw the girl.

The teenager was peering at them from behind an arbutus tree. The moment she realised Sara had spotted her she slipped out of sight, elusive as a forest nymph.

A leggy little thing, Sara mused, and pretty—except for the unfortunate haircut!

'You're smiling,' Zach said. 'What's up?'

'Oh…that girl. I saw her…but she's gone now.'

'Probably the last you'll see of her.' Zach put his hand in the small of her back and nudged her inside the cottage. 'Young kid like that…what could she find to interest her in a couple of old fogeys like us?'

Next morning, the sound of a motor boat woke Logan.

He grunted, flung his arms out over the mattress, and squinted at his bedside clock.

It wasn't even six! Who the devil was making that racket before the birds had even started their dawn chorus?

Flinging himself out of bed, he stumbled, naked,

across to the window overlooking the Straits, and yanked
up the venetian blinds.

Eyes still bleary with sleep, he peered out. And
blinked when he saw that the white cabin cruiser was
no longer tied up at the dock. It was heading away fast
in the direction of the mainland.

Deep satisfaction immediately followed his initial moment of surprise—deep satisfaction and a relish that was
almost malicious. Had the cabin been too spartan for
Zach Grant's sybaritic tastes? Or had it been the haughty
blonde who had found its shabby bareness intolerable?
Whatever—Logan ran his fingers through his tousled
hair and grinned—they were gone.

Hallelujah!

Fired with a sudden burst of energy, he crossed to the
bathroom and snatched up a pair of swimming trunks
from the towel rail. He'd go down there right now and
remove their garbage—people like them *always* left garbage: empty bottles, unwashed glasses, overflowing ash-
trays, soiled sheets...and worse. Contempt curled his upper lip.

Afterwards, he'd go for a swim off the dock.

The water would be icy; but it might help wash away
his feeling of profound distaste at the thought of the
cottage having been used as a love nest.

Sara had planned to return to her bed after seeing Zach
off, but by the time she'd walked back to the cottage
from the jetty the chilly morning air had slapped her
wide awake.

So instead she made for the smaller bedroom which
Zach had used; she tore the linen off the bed, packed
the blankets away, and, after tidying up the room, tossed
the sheets and pillow slips into the bathroom hamper.

Then she was about to step into the shower, when she changed her mind. She'd soak in a long and lazy bath...and then she'd make herself another pot of coffee.

It was wonderful, she reflected as she turned on the taps and slipped out of her robe, to be on holiday. To have no worries; no deadlines; no plans of any kind.

And the best thing about this particular holiday was that she was going to spend it absolutely on her own.

As for that hateful man in the white house on the hill, she would just ignore him, pretend he didn't exist.

It was the only way to deal with people like him!

Logan stuck the key in the lock, turned the knob, and pushed the door open.

The interior of the cottage was silent. The only sounds came from outside. Birds warbled, dancing wavelets splashed against the jetty, the brisk breeze rustled leaves in the garden. He left the door open and stepped inside.

The air was dusty, with the faint lingering smell of coffee. So...they'd breakfasted before they'd gone.

He moved through to the kitchen, and snorted with disgust. Just as he'd expected, they'd left the place a pigsty. Hadn't even emptied the coffeepot; hadn't even cleared the table, far less washed the mugs and plates.

He'd start cleaning in here, but first he'd check to see what kind of a mess they'd left in the other areas.

He poked his nose into the smaller bedroom and saw that the mattress was bare. He assumed the couple had used the larger room, with its double bed, and, when he checked it out, saw that his assumption had been correct.

Slobs.

The sheets were on the floor, as were the tumbled blankets. They'd had some kind of a wild night, he thought as he glowered at the bed.

And if they'd left the bedroom like this he could only imagine what was awaiting him in the bathroom.

He strode down the narrow hallway, took a deep breath...and flung the door open.

CHAPTER TWO

SARA screamed.

Lost in daydreams and pampered to the chin in gardenia-scented bath bubbles, she had drifted off to sleep. Now, as the door crashed inwards, with her scream shrilling in her ears, she shot up to a sitting position. And with her heart in her mouth she stared with horrified disbelief and fast-rising panic at the figure in the doorway. She'd always felt nature had dealt her a generous hand in the courage department; now she felt terror squeeze that courage down to the size and consistency of a mini-marshmallow!

Logan Hunter.

Man on the prowl.

Naked man on the prowl!

No, not naked; he *was* wearing swimming trunks—but they were the same brown as his skin so her error had been understandable. She gulped back the lump that almost closed her throat. His black hair was dishevelled, his jaw dark-stubbled, and his eyes were fixed, with the blank look of a person hypnotised, on the foam frothing up over her breasts.

Sex. He wanted sex. He'd seen Zach leave and had lost no time in coming after her! The man was a raving maniac!

'Get out!' she shrieked. Snatching the heavy glass bottle of bubble beads from the rack at her elbow, she threw it wildly at him. She missed by a country mile. It smashed against the wall and clattered unbroken to the floor.

'Get out,' she screeched, 'you nasty, disgusting old pervert—' She scooped up the giant-sized cake of Heavenly Gardenia soap from the edge of the bath and rocketed it at his face. Her aim was atrocious, but he dodged, and the hard oval bar met his brow with a crack that made him wince.

'Ouch!' He staggered back a step. 'Cut it out.'

To her dismay, she noticed that the bath bubbles had started to deflate. Frantically she threshed the dying suds with the flat of her hands in an attempt to revive them, but in vain. The water had cooled, and the bubbles only grew smaller and smaller, concealed her less and less...

With a quavering moan, she slid down as far as she could go without submerging herself fully, and prayed that the few remaining bubbles would continue to act as a veil.

'I'll drown myself!' she moaned, splaying her hands over her breasts and almost throwing out her back as she twisted her crossed legs away from him. 'I'll drown myself, I *swear*, rather than give in to you and your wicked—'

'Give *in* to me?' His curse turned the air blue. 'Lady, you're out of your mind. I saw the boat leave and I merely came down to see what Zach Grant had left behind. What I certainly didn't expect to find was...you.' He crossed to the mirror above the sink, swiped a hand over the glass to clear the steam, and leaned forward to inspect his brow. 'You just missed my eye,' he accused. 'Lucky for you—' he turned '—or I'd have sued the *pants* off you...'

His gaze trailed from her face to her body, and he

raised a cynical brow. 'But I guess,' he added mock-ingly, 'they're already off.'

Sara felt a sheet of heat skim from her neck to the tips of her toes. She had no idea how much of her was visible through the scanty remaining foam—but she'd have walked barefoot over white-hot coals rather than give this man the satisfaction of seeing her peek to check.

'All right.' She tilted her chin regally. 'Please leave now. Your explanation and apology are accepted—'

'Apology?' he sputtered. 'What apology? You're the one who should be doing the apologising—'

A loud hammering on the front door stopped him short.

'Hello?' The voice was high-pitched, nervous, young. 'Anyone in there? Is everything OK?'

Sara saw him roll his eyes.

'My daughter!' He raked a hand through his already mussed black hair, his expression that of an animal caught in a leghold trap. 'Where angels fear to tread, she just barges in—'

'Like father, like daughter!' Sara's courage had swelled up again, but too late to give her any feeling of pride or pleasure.

'I guess.' The faintest twinkle gleamed in his eyes.

Green eyes. Sara had noticed that when she'd first met him. Then, and moments ago, they'd been cold and hos-tile. Now, for the first time, she saw a glimmer of warmth, and it kindled an odd spark of excitement deep inside her.

'For God's sake—' his voice was hoarse '—don't tell her about this. I'll never hear the end of it.'

Without waiting for an answer, he wheeled away, slamming the bathroom door behind him.

Sara slumped, boneless as a drunken jellyfish. Her body trembled; her heart trembled. If that confrontation was a portent of the kind of holiday that lay ahead, perhaps it would indeed have been better if Zach had rented her a de luxe condo in a busy holiday resort...

'What happened, Dad?' The girl's voice drifted into the bathroom through the open window as father and daughter walked along the side of the cottage. 'I heard the scream and I ran to your room to see if you had too, but you weren't there, so I guessed you must have come down to investigate.'

Sara held her breath, curious to hear Logan's answer.

'It was nothing, sweetie. Zach Grant's gone—his girlfriend's here on her own, and apparently when she was in the bathroom she saw a...mouse.'

The voices faded, and once again Sara relaxed.

A mouse. No, Mr Logan, she disdainfully corrected him, what I saw in my bathroom was certainly not a mouse.

It looked *much* more like a rat.

'After we finish breakfast, I'm going to start clearing out your mother's things from the master bedroom.' Logan watched his daughter carefully from across the verandah table, alert to any sign of distress. 'Care to help?'

Andy's huge brown eyes gave nothing away as they met his. 'No, that's OK, Dad. You should probably do it on your own. I'll start packing up the books in the den. Where are the boxes?'

'Should be a bunch up in the attic. We'll get them later.'

Andy nodded and, bending her head over her bowl, dug her spoon into her cereal.

Logan felt a wave of weariness wash over him. Andy

was a real trooper and he was so proud of her he sometimes could hardly contain it…but he wished now, as he
so often did, that she weren't so adept at keeping her
emotions under control. Apart from an outburst of hysterical sobbing when her mother had died, she'd never
let go. Not once. At least, not in front of him. If she
cried, she cried alone.

In the beginning, he'd tried to talk to her about her
Mom, but in the end had given up. She was as closed
as a clam. It would have helped her, he felt sure, if they
could have shared their sorrow. And it would have
helped him too.

Another problem was that everybody they knew
avoided talking about Bethany. They probably thought
they were being kind, but it would have been more natural to remember her aloud, to recall all the wonderful
things about her.

Sometimes it seemed to him as if his beloved wife
had never existed…except in his own life.

'That was a big sigh, Dad,' Andy murmured. 'What's
up?'

'Oh…it's…' he searched his brain for an answer that
would satisfy her '…um…just that woman in the cottage, sweetie—I want you to keep away from her.'

He got up from the table and, shoving his hands into
his pockets, looked down at his daughter. Her hair was
damp from her shower, and the sun caught copper highlights in the ragged strands. His heart ached as he remembered how Bethany's long brown hair had glinted
in just such a way…

'Why, Dad?'

'Why what?'

Andy uttered a sound of exasperation. 'Why must I
keep away from "that woman"?'

She said 'that woman' in a tone of dark melodrama, which Logan chose to ignore. 'Because, daughter mine, rightly or wrongly, society judges people by the company they keep. I want you to stick with people whose values are the same as your own. A good reputation's worth its weight in gold—and it's something you can lose only once.'

'Kind of like virginity, right, Dad?'

Logan cleared his throat, and busied himself with gathering up his dishes. 'Right,' he said. 'Darned right.'

A feeling of helplessness and inadequacy almost swamped him. He was no good at this; he was clumsy, awkward—or, to use Andy's latest expression of derision, 'pathetic'.

She needed a mother, especially at this stage in her life, where she was herself on the threshold of womanhood. And he *did* intend to take himself another wife...but only because of his promise to Bethany.

Just the memory of it broke his heart.

'Darling,' she'd whispered as she'd lain dying in the stark white hospital bed, 'promise me you'll marry again.' Her voice had caught. 'I couldn't bear it if I thought you'd go through the rest of your life grieving...'

He'd have promised her the moon if he'd thought it would give her a moment's respite from her suffering.

'I promise—' the lump in his throat had almost choked him '—if that's what you want, I'll marry again...'

And the promise had been worth it, to see the quick shine of relief in her dulled eyes, to feel the tiny surge of strength in the fragile fingers clutching his.

He'd had to turn away to hide his tears.

Five years had passed since he'd made that promise.

Five long years, and his failure to honour it weighed on him more heavily with each passing day.

No more.

He'd sworn to himself that this summer he'd find himself a wife.

She'd have to be someone Andy liked.

She'd have to be someone he himself found compatible.

She'd have to be someone sensible. Someone with no frilly romantic notions. Someone willing to enter into a marriage of convenience.

He felt a dark cloud of despair settle over him as he carried his dishes into the house.

Where the hell would he find somebody like that?

Marriage to Travis Wynter had stifled Sara's creativity. Had all but killed it.

It hadn't happened straight away, but it had *started* to happen soon after the honeymoon.

Unhappy memories flowed into Sara's mind as she tugged the last item from her travel bag—an elegant silk and rayon sweater of turquoise and silver, with the trademark Sally Cole label hand-sewn inside the back neckline.

Her label.

Her design.

Her pride.

She sighed, and ran a gentle hand over the soft fabric. Her marriage had been a mistake; she and Travis had been totally wrong for each other. His possessiveness, the way he'd treated her like an item in his collection of beautiful artifacts...well, that had been one thing... but his dismissal of her talent had been another.

Travis was an accountant; he saw life in terms of facts

and figures. His favourite expression was 'the bottom line'. And she'd discovered, to her dismay, that where their marriage was concerned 'the bottom line' was that he expected her to run his home the way he ran his business: efficiently and economically. He'd seen no reason to hire a housekeeper when he had a wife. He'd entertained clients at home on a regular basis, and on those occasions he'd expected her to cook the meal, serve it, and be the perfect hostess. And he'd expected the enormous Wynter house, in Vancouver's glitziest suburb, to be kept in immaculate condition.

If he'd seen as much as one mote of dust on the furniture, his disapproval had been swift and harsh.

'For God's sake, Sara, what do you do all day? All I ask is that you keep house and provide meals for my clients. Make them feel special. How special do you think they feel when they see you haven't even dusted the damned coffee table before they turned up? This is *business*—'

'But my designs, my knitwear—that's business too,' she'd protested vigorously in the beginning. 'I'm not going to give it up!'

'Nobody's asking you to give it up. Just for God's sake get things in perspective. Could we survive on the income from your little sweaters? I think not. The bottom line is, I'm the breadwinner here. If you want to draw and knit, go ahead. But *after* everything else gets done, mmm?'

His business had been prospering by leaps and bounds, and before very long Sara had found, wearily, that there was no 'after'. And even if there had been his cold dismissal of her work had shrivelled something inside her.

Life with Travis Wynter had allowed no room for that soaring of the spirit that she needed if she were to create.

She'd wondered, sometimes—and still wondered—if he had not only stifled her creativity, but had killed it.

Inhaling a deep breath, she rose from the bed and slung the lightweight sweater over her shoulders. On her way to the bedroom door, she paused as a movement outside the window caught her attention.

It was the girl from the white house—Logan Hunter's daughter. She was running down the sloping lawn, towards the cottage.

What could she want?

Sara walked along the narrow passageway to the front door, and opened it. The girl was now just a few feet away, coming up the path. She stopped abruptly when she saw Sara.

'Hi,' Sara greeted her, and thought, What a lovely child…huge brown eyes, smooth clear skin, neat little figure…but oh, that hair! 'Were you looking for me?'

The girl's cheeks had turned pink, and she seemed on the point of flight.

'I was up in the attic,' she said in a rush, 'looking for boxes…for packing…and I found this.'

'This' was a mouse trap! Somehow Sara managed to keep her face straight. 'Just what I need!' She took the trap, gave a dainty shiver. 'I'm such a coward when it comes to mice. A lion, now…if I saw one of those in the bathroom, I'd just grab a back scrubber and attack with gusto!'

The girl giggled. 'Oh, yeah, sure…'

'Would you like to come in…have a cup of coffee?'

'I don't drink coffee.'

'Iced tea, then, or a pop?'

'No, thanks.' Her gaze trailed wistfully over Sara's

sweater. 'That's a Sally Cole original, isn't it? They're way cool...my friend Chrissie's mom has one; she bought it years ago but she says you can't get them any more.' She sighed. 'Well, I'd better get back...'

'Ah, yes, the packing.'

'We're going to sell. The house and the cottage. Everything. My dad's putting the property up for sale.'

'I guess you're in a hurry to go back and help him, then. Many hands make light work, don't they say?'

'Well, he's upstairs and I'm not actually helping him this morning. He's clearing out Mom's things—I thought he'd want to do that on his own.'

A chill prickled Sara's nape as she heard the catch in the young voice, saw the quickly blinked-back tears in the luminous brown eyes. She wanted to reach out to the child, but without warning the slight figure whirled away and ran off, taking a short cut over an overgrown rosebed. To Sara's horror, she tripped on a tangled root, and fell forward, to land in a crumpled heap on the ground.

Sara rushed to help her get up, but as the girl put her weight on her right foot she winced and grabbed onto Sara for support.

'I've done something to my ankle,' she said with a half-sob. 'It really hurts.'

'Come inside and—'

'Thanks...but I'd rather go home. Will you help me walk back? I don't think I can do it on my own.'

'Of course. Here, put your arm around my neck.' Sara grimaced. 'I haven't even asked you your name,' she said as she braced herself to support the slender figure.

'It's Andrea. Andrea Beth Hunter.'

'Andrea. That's pretty. I'm Sara Wynter.'

'Miss Wynter, I—'

'It's Mrs Wynter, actually, but please call me Sara.'

They started up towards the house, with Andrea hopping erratically on her left leg, and leaning heavily on Sara.

'Mrs Wynter, I...um...saw you with Zach Grant.'

Sara hid a smile as she heard the wistful note in Andrea's voice. So...a fan. 'Yes, he brought me here. I wish he could've stayed longer, but he's—'

'He's filming in Vancouver. I know. My friend Chrissie and I—we're members of his fan club. Will he...be coming back?'

'He'll be coming to pick me up in a couple of weeks. Then shortly after he'll be returning to Los Angeles. He lives there...but of course—' Sara smiled '—you'll already know that.'

She was heading for the front door, but Andrea said, 'Let's use the side door. I don't want Dad to hear me come in...if he sees me hopping like this...well, he's a regular old fusspot!'

'But you'll have to tell him about your ankle—'

'Oh, I will. But first I'll put an ice pack on it. There's a bag of green peas in the freezer; I'll use that.'

On reaching the side door, Sara tugged it open, and they entered what turned out to be a small sitting room.

'The kitchen's across the hall from here,' Andrea said.

Sara noticed her face had become very white. 'Come sit down on this sofa and put your leg up while I get the ice.'

After a token protest, Andrea allowed herself to be helped onto the sofa, where she lay back, her eyes closed. 'There's a bottle of aspirin in one of the drawers,' she said huskily. 'Could you bring me a couple?'

'Of course.'

From above came the sound of someone moving about.

'That's Dad,' Andrea offered with a weak gesture of one hand. 'He's packing in the master bedroom. Like I said...' Her voice trailed away.

Sara hurried to the kitchen, and found the bag of peas in the freezer section of the fridge. Locating the aspirin wasn't so easy. She pulled out drawer after drawer, riffled through the tidy contents of each one, and had reached the last, in a cabinet at the far end of the kitchen, when she heard Logan Hunter's voice come from the doorway behind her.

'What the hell,' he said in a tone of quiet menace, 'are you doing in my house?'

She put a hand to her throat as she swivelled round, and threw him a shaky smile. 'You startled me! I'm just looking for—'

'What you're looking for, and what you're going to get, lady, is trouble. You'll find nothing else here. I don't keep money stashed in the kitchen, and if you're looking for drugs in that medicine cabinet you've come to the wrong place—'

'Daddy!' Horror filled the voice that came from behind Logan. 'Don't! Mrs Wynter came to help me—'

Sara looked beyond Logan as he spun round, and saw Andy hopping along the carpeted hallway in her bare feet, bracing her hand against the wall with each jerky hop.

'Andy? What the—?' Logan sounded shocked.

'I fell, Dad, and twisted my ankle, or sprained it or something. I had to ask Mrs Wynter to help me back to the house, and then she offered to get me an ice bag and some aspirin.' Face ashen, Andrea started to slump, and would have slid to the floor if her father hadn't moved fast.

He scooped her up in his arms and, muttering under his breath, took off with her in the direction of the small sitting room, leaving Sara standing alone in the kitchen, feeling limp as a wet rag herself.

Her hand shook as she put the aspirin bottle on the countertop. It shook as she set down the frozen peas beside the aspirin. And by the time she had poured a glass of cold water from the tap, and placed it by the peas, her whole body was trembling.

The man, she decided with a rising tide of anger, was an ogre...and he *certainly* didn't deserve to have a daughter as sweet as Andrea.

She hoped the child was going to be all right.

But, either way, she herself was going to avoid both father and daughter, for the rest of her time on the island.

And if that turned out to be impossible she'd place a call to Zach and ask him to come back early and pick her up.

No way would her creative juices ever have a chance to start flowing again as long as Logan Hunter was around.

The thought added fuel to her anger, and resentment burned to her very bones as she let herself out by the kitchen door and stomped back down the hill to the cottage.

CHAPTER THREE

Just before noon, Sara heard heavy footsteps outside the bathroom window and recognised Logan Hunter's purposeful tread.

What did he want this time?

And his timing couldn't have been worse, she decided as she glanced ruefully down at her skimpily clad figure!

She jumped when she heard his loud rat-tat-tat on the front door.

Wrapping a huge terry towel around herself, over her undies, she padded barefoot out of the bathroom, and was halfway along the passage when he knocked again.

She stopped at the closed door and spoke through it. 'What do you want?' Her tone was frosty.

'I want to talk to you.'

'This is not a good time.'

She listened. There was no sound of retreating feet. Heaving out a frustrated sigh, she leaned back against the door and looked down the narrow hallway to the living room. A dingy little room. And bare as a baby's bottom. Minimum amount of furniture...sofa, two armchairs, one coffee table, one ancient TV. 'I said,' she threw into the hallway, 'this is not a good time.'

'Then I'll wait here till it is. What I want to say has to be said.'

'Through the door, then.'

'To your face.'

'Sorry, but—'

He shoved the door open and sent her flying down the passage. She only just managed to keep her balance, but as she scrambled to stay upright the towel became dislodged, caught under her feet and she tripped. Flailing in the air, she fell against the wall with a sideways thud that jarred her shoulder and knocked the breath out of her.

Logan Hunter loomed over her, his arms outstretched in an offer of help that wasn't only too late, but also unwelcome.

'You,' she gasped, 'are a menace!' She snatched up her towel and breathlessly wrapped it around herself...but not before he'd treated himself to a good eyeful of every creamy curve! Resentment swept through her with the steaming heat of tropical rain.

'Hey,' he protested, 'how was I expected to know you were leaning against the—?'

'What right do you think you have to push your way in here as if you owned the place...?' She halted, jolted by the sudden stunned expression in his eyes. 'What's the...?'

'You're green,' he choked out. 'What in the world happened to you? Are you sick?'

He staggered back against the opposite wall as if the very sight of her had knocked the knees from under him.

'All right,' she snapped, 'say what you have to say then get out.'

'It's a face mask.' He ran a hand over his mouth, and she was sure he was hiding a smile. 'Ruined now, of course. Cracked all to hell.' The smile couldn't be contained. It became a chuckle. And then a full-bodied belly laugh. 'Hey, I'm sorry...but if you could only see yourself—'

'Say what you have to say,' she gritted, 'and get out of here!' *Out of my life!*

'First of all, then—' his voice had a strangled sound '—I came in here as if I owned the place because I *do* own the place.'

'When it's rented out, you have absolutely no right whatsoever to come in here without an invitation.'

'Which you were not about to offer, as I recall—'

'Nor ever will! OK, that's the "First of all" taken care of. Now, what was the real point of your visit?'

'I came to apologise.'

'For...?'

'For...assuming the worst this morning. For accusing you without asking for your side of the story. I assure you it won't ever happen again.'

For a second, she melted. He looked so sincerely repentant, she was almost on the point of forgiving him. And then she heard a muffled moan come from deep in his throat, and she knew he was laughing at her. Again.

'Get out!' Temper aflare, she jerked the towel even more tightly around her breasts to make doubly sure it wouldn't fall again as she marched back along the hall to the door, which still lay open.

She stalked to one side, bracing herself, waiting for him to pass by.

'I think,' he said softly, 'it would be a good idea if, from now on, you and I could keep out of each other's way.'

'Oh, you'll get no argument from me on that point, Mr Hunter. I couldn't agree more.'

'Well, hell, finally we've agreed on something. Who says miracles don't happen?'

He grinned, and the sight infuriated her. She wanted

to slap him, but she stood still as a marble statue, refusing to give him the satisfaction of seeing how close to being out of control she really was.

He left then. And as he brushed past her his arm touched hers. She hadn't been expecting that, nor could she possibly have anticipated the shock of electricity that passed between them. It jolted her whole body and she inhaled sharply. With the inhalation came the musky scent of him.

It was heady, and intoxicating, and erotic.

She stared after him, her legs sagging, her mind reeling, as he strode away along the path.

She couldn't have moved had her life depended on it.

She was still standing there, rooted to the floor, long after he'd disappeared around the corner.

She'd never felt such a thing before. Oh, she'd read about it, but she'd never experienced it—that sexual electricity that could arc between a man and a woman.

It was disturbing…it was exhilarating.

And it was the very last thing in the world she wanted.

Over the next week, Logan saw next to nothing of his near-neighbour…but that didn't mean he didn't think about her.

He didn't *want* to think about her, but from time to time, when he least expected it, images of her would sneak into his mind.

Two images, to be exact.

The first invariably set his pulses pounding: the fiery Mrs Wynter wearing nothing but a white cotton bra and bikini panties, her skin so smooth it just begged to be caressed.

The second…well, even now he couldn't think of it

without chuckling. She'd looked like an alien from Mars with that green face mask...but with those turquoise eyes spitting at him and those pink lips snapping at him and that glorious blonde hair scraped back in a perky ponytail she'd been something else again...

Only what that something else was he couldn't pin down. And he didn't even begin to try to.

The woman spelled trouble, with every letter in bold black caps!

His decision to stay away from her was one of the most sensible he'd ever made in his life.

And on this sunny afternoon, as he walked into his study, he idly congratulated himself on that very thing. Life on the island had always been simple, and he wanted to keep it that way. No complications, no entanglements.

'Andy—' he hitched a hip on the edge of the computer desk, where his daughter was sitting at the keyboard '—I thought I'd take a hike to the old swimming hole and cool off. Want to come?'

'No, thanks, Dad.' Andrea's eyes were fixed on the monitor. 'I've got tons of e-mail to answer. You go, though. I'll catch you later.'

'Fan club stuff?'

'Mmm...'

'OK.' He glanced around. 'Can't believe we've been here a week, but we've gotten a pile of work done...though this room looks so darned bare now without all our books. The whole house looks bare, with all the knick-knacks packed away—'

'Dad, do you mind? I'm leaving with Chrissie tomorrow morning...I've really got to get these letters written this afternoon.'

He pushed himself to his feet. 'Right, I'll be off. What are we having for dinner?'

'Oh, it's my turn, isn't it?' Finally, she looked up at him, but in an absent way, with a distracted frown tucking her brows together. 'How about…um…a stir-fry?'

Her mother's eyes. Large, the colour of rich dark chocolate, fringed with thick sable lashes. Just looking into them sent his thoughts spinning backwards. The ache of his loss…would it never go away? He'd always known he was a one-woman man; what he hadn't known was the price he'd have to pay for being that way…

'Stir-fry it is.' He set a light hand on his daughter's shoulder. 'Did I ever tell you you're a great kid?'

'Did I ever tell you you're a great dad?'

Under his palm, he felt her shoulder muscles tighten. Her eyes lost their vague expression and became focused, serious. Determined.

'We're a team, right?' she said.

He tried to lighten the moment. 'Oh, sure…till some Prince Charming comes along and whisks you away on the back of his white charger—'

'No way!' She surged up from her chair and gave him a fierce hug. 'I'll *never* leave you, Dad. That's one thing you'll never have to worry about. I don't want a Prince Charming. I don't need anybody else but you. We don't need anybody else but each other. For ever.'

When Logan left the house a few minutes later, his mood was troubled. And it remained that way as he followed the track through the woods to the swimming hole. How come he'd never noticed before just how dependent on him Andy had become? Sure, they spent a lot of time together; he'd made a point of doing that; he'd tried to fill the space her mother had left in her life.

But he hadn't realised the intensity of her dependence on him. He hadn't realised that there was a possessive aspect to her feelings for him.

If ignored, it could eventually become unhealthy. He had to put a stop to it. Without delay.

He was still thinking about the problem half an hour later, when he heard the sound of rushing water ahead. Veering off the track, he cut through the undergrowth, and made his way to the six-foot-high rock east of the fall.

Shedding his shirt and trainers, he ambled round the rock, and dived into the crystal clear waters of the pool.

Sara started as she heard the sound of splashing. Not the steady rush of the waterfall, but a more erratic sound.

She pushed herself up on her elbows and squinted against the sun. She'd come upon the swimming hole by accident days ago, and had spent her afternoons there ever since. Afternoons that had been peaceful and un-interrupted. But now... She frowned as she saw that the surface of the swimming hole was rippled.

Someone surged to the surface, and her heart lurched. It was a man. With dark hair.

She sprang to her feet, and slipped behind the huge granite rock at her side. Peeking round warily, pulses racing, she waited.

The swimmer shot to the surface again. And started swimming lethargically around the large pool. He was wearing brief trunks...the same colour as his hide.

Logan Hunter.

Frustration burned like bile in her throat. Was there no getting away from the man? She'd come all this way to avoid him…and here he was, like the proverbial bad penny!

She drew back behind the rock again, and that was when she noticed his shirt and sneakers. He'd tossed them down there, quite unaware that anyone else was around.

Her eyes narrowed. A wicked smile twitched the corners of her mouth. He'd called her a thief, hadn't he? Well, give a dog a bad name, might as well hang it!

It took her just a moment to gather up her own things and put them in her backpack; then she scooped up his shirt and sneakers.

It's going to be a long walk home, Mr Hunter!

Laughter bubbled up inside her as she snuck away.

'Gotcha!'

Sara gasped, and Logan's shirt and shoes tumbled from her hands.

Logan took enormous delight in having startled the devious Mrs Wynter as he grasped her shoulders. He whirled her round and he couldn't keep the smugness from his expression as he looked down into her shocked face.

Her cheeks were bright pink. 'I thought—'

'You thought I wouldn't see you.' What kind of perfume was she wearing? Something tangy, provocative… 'But I did. And now you're going to have to pay.'

'Pay?' she asked faintly.

'You didn't think you could plot to make me hike two miles in my bare feet…and get away with it?' he mocked.

'It was a joke.'

'Ah. A joke.'

'Well—' she tilted her nose up at him defiantly '—not so much a joke as…retribution.'

'For…?'

'For calling me a thief.'

'I apologised for that.'

'It still stings.'

She tried to wrench free, but he only held her arms tighter. 'Not as much as my feet would have stung if I'd had to walk home with no shoes.' She looked breathless; her chest was rising and falling rapidly, and her glorious turquoise eyes were dilated. On her brow, almost hidden by the sweep of her blonde hair, was a tiny indentation. The kind of mark left by chicken pox. He wanted to kiss it…

'Well, you won't have to suffer now,' she said. 'So would you mind letting me go? I want—'

She broke off, and he saw her swallow. 'Yes?' His voice had become husky. 'What do you want?'

The pink tingeing her cheeks had darkened to a vibrant scarlet. 'I want you to stop…looking at me like that.'

He raised his brows. 'Like what?'

'As if you're…wondering how it would feel to…kiss me.'

'Mind-reader, huh?'

'No, just…a woman.' She flicked a quick look at his bare chest, which gleamed wet from the pool. Nervously, she ran the tip of her tongue over her upper lip.

She'd been right; he'd wanted to kiss her. But now, as he watched that moist pink tongue move where he'd wanted his own lips to move, he wanted a whole lot more.

But a kiss would be a good place to start.

He drove his cool, damp hands into her hair and swept it right back from her face. Then he clasped her head with his long fingers, holding her fast.

For a long moment they stared into each other's eyes, and sexual excitement shimmered between them like the gossamer flutter of a butterfly's wings.

'You're wondering too,' he said softly, and, sliding a hand from her hair, traced a fingertip over her lip, where her tongue had been. He felt the faint tremble of the moist flesh, and found it incredibly arousing.

Her lashes fluttered closed, as if she couldn't bear to look at him, couldn't bear the electricity crackling back and forth between them.

'Tell me,' he whispered, now tracing his fingertip over the fine curve of her jaw. 'Tell me you're wondering too.'

A small moan was her only answer. He lowered his head, and water from his hair dropped onto the thin cotton of her shirt, making it cling in places to her breasts. His throat almost closed as lust catapulted him from tenderness to urgency. Male hormones amok. Testosterone on the rampage.

With a ragged groan, he dragged her against his wet body. And kissed her. Desperately.

The taste of her lips was even more lusciously sweet than he'd anticipated, the silky texture something close to heaven. He deepened the kiss, and heard her whimper. He stepped her backwards towards the tree behind her. She sagged weakly against it, and he slid his mouth along her jaw to the sensitive spot below her ear.

'Still with me?' he whispered against her scented skin.

She slid her arms around his neck, clung there as if her legs had become too weak to support her. 'That—'

her voice was blurred, like velvet rubbed the wrong way '—is a loaded question—'

'*Daddy!*'

The appalled voice came from behind him.

He froze…and felt Sara stiffen. Then she snatched her arms from around his neck and pushed him from her.

Oh, God, he thought despairingly—Andy! Where had she come from, and what was she doing here?

Heartbeats jamming, he turned.

His daughter was ten feet away. She was wearing jeans over a red and white spotted swimsuit, and she had a red towel slung over her shoulder. Her hair stood up in jagged little curls, and her face was whiter than the snowy foam at the foot of the waterfall.

'Sweetie—' Logan heard the choking sound in his own voice '—what are you doing here? I thought you were going to be busy with your letters—'

'How could you, Daddy?' The huge brown eyes were filled to the brim with tears. She didn't once let her gaze flit to Sara; kept it fixed, agonisedly, on him. 'Oh, how could you?'

'Honey—'

'I followed you. I thought you were lonely. I felt sorry for you, after you'd gone, so I came after you. But all the time you knew I was busy and you were planning to meet—'

'No, no, Andy.' He stepped towards her. 'It's not what you think—'

'Oh, spare me!' She stumbled back, her gaze now more anguished than ever. 'You're a *hypocrite*, Dad. You told me to keep away from her—"that woman", you called her! You told me you're judged by the company you keep, and you said—you said…a person's reputation…is…'

The words ended in a wail, and her face crumpled. Blindly, roughly, she brushed at her over-spilling tears. 'Oh, I hate you,' she sobbed. 'I just *hate* you.'

She spun around and took off along the trail, back the way she'd come. Her sneakers kicked up spurts of dry dirt with each step, leaving faint dusty clouds in the air.

Logan stood, as if too stunned to move.

'Go after her.' Shakily, Sara folded her arms around herself. 'Hurry.'

He jolted to life. Shoving his feet into his trainers, he fastened the laces, and grabbed his shirt. About to leave, he glanced at her, his eyes dark. Unhappy. 'You'll be OK?'

She nodded.

'Sure?'

'Go.'

After a brief hesitation, he did as she bade. He took off, fast, his steps thudding hard on the sun-baked trail.

Sara stood where she was till he was out of sight, and the sound of his steps had faded away.

Only then did she hitch her backpack more firmly over her shoulders, and start the long trek home.

'Sweetie—' Logan tapped on his daughter's bedroom door '— you can't stay locked in there for ever. And hey—' he tried for a touch of humour '—I'm starving…it's almost seven o'clock. What about that stir-fry you promised?'

No answer.

He muttered frustratedly under his breath. He'd soon caught up with Andy that afternoon, on the trail from the swimming hole, but she'd refused to listen to him. And when they'd reached the house she'd raced furiously upstairs and slammed the bedroom door in his face.

She hadn't come out since, despite his repeated efforts to coax her to unlock the door.

He sighed, and was about to turn away, when he heard her call, sulkily, 'The door's not locked.'

It had been, earlier. His spirits rose a notch.

He opened the door and walked into the room.

She was sitting cross-legged on the bed, with a book spread out on her lap.

She didn't look up.

'Let's clear the air,' he said quietly, and crossed to the cushioned wicker chair by the bed. He sat down, and grasped the curved arms of the chair. 'Andy...?'

'What?' She still didn't look up, but now he could see that her eyes were red-rimmed, the lids swollen. He resisted the urge to reach out to her. She wasn't ready for that yet; her body was rigid with hostility, every taut line of her young face screamed defiance.

'Have I ever lied to you?'

Her lower lip jutted out, and she shrugged.

'Please answer me.'

She picked at a scab on her knee. 'I guess not,' she said sulkily.

'Yes or no?'

'No,' she muttered.

'OK.' He relaxed—a little. 'So here's what happened. I went to the swimming hole, alone, expecting to be there alone. I didn't see Mrs Wynter; she must have been sunning herself on the grass at the far side of the rock. At any rate, when I was in the water, she stole my shoes and shirt...but I spotted her. I chased after her, and grabbed her...'

Andy was looking at him now, her eyes gleaming. 'She was going to make you walk home in your bare feet?'

'Yeah.'

He could see she was trying not to smile. 'Go on.'

'Well,' he said, 'what happened next...' He cleared his throat.

'The kiss.'

He met her gaze squarely. 'That's the hard part to explain. I was darned annoyed at her for disturbing my swim. I guess I wanted to...well, show her!'

'Dad—' Andy cupped her hands around her knees and fixed him with an oddly adult gaze '—I sometimes think you're living in the Dark Ages. If you kissed Mrs Wynter against her will, you'll be lucky if she doesn't sue you for sexual harassment. That would teach you a lesson.'

She scrambled off the bed, and, tucking her arm through his, looked seriously up into his face. 'But I don't think she will. She probably wouldn't want Zach Grant to know she'd been kissing anybody else. But the best thing would be for you to keep right away from her. Keep your distance, Dad. Play it safe.'

'That's very good advice,' Logan muttered. 'And I intend to follow it to the letter.'

Next morning, Sara woke around eight. She was in the kitchen, enjoying a mug of freshly brewed coffee at the kitchen table, when she heard the throb of an engine.

When she looked out of the window, she saw a luxurious silver craft coming alongside the jetty. Three peo-

ple were on deck: a couple, and a fair-haired girl about
Andy's age.

A movement closer at hand drew her attention, and,
turning her head, she saw Logan and his daughter walking down the beach. The teenager was wearing a backpack.

As Sara watched, the fair-haired girl leaped onto the
dock and with a scream of excitement ran to greet Andy,
squealing with surprise over Andy's cropped hair.
Logan, after pausing to exchange a few words with the
girl, ambled on and stopped alongside the craft.

The adults chatted for a minute, and then the two girls
boarded the vessel, but not before Andy had hugged
Logan.

The morning was quiet, the kitchen window open, and
she heard him call, 'See y'all in a couple of days. Bye,
Andy.'

'Bye, Dad...'

It would seem, Sara mused with a wry smile, that
Andy had forgiven her father his trespasses of the previous day!

As Logan walked back along the floating dock, he
chanced to glance at the cottage, and saw 'that woman'
peering out at him from behind a tugged-aside curtain
in the kitchen window.

As soon as she realised he'd spotted her, she dropped
the curtain like a red-hot coal and disappeared from
sight.

Logan cursed under his breath. What a mistake that
kiss had been. She'd be having all sorts of ideas about

him now. Damage control, he decided, was what was called for now. And there was no point in putting it off.

Wheeling around sharply, he squared his shoulders and strode determinedly towards the cottage.

CHAPTER FOUR

SARA opened the door at Logan's knock, and faced him.

'Yes?' She clutched her hand more tightly around her coffee mug; in his unshaven state and with his black hair mussed he looked so appealing, she wanted to reach out and touch him. 'What can I do for you?'

His gaze was belligerent. 'I just wanted to let you know that I sorted things out with my daughter. Yesterday. Last night. Regarding the…regarding our… um…'

She raised her brows but offered nothing to help him out.

He glowered. 'The…um…kiss. It…threw her.'

'Understandably so. The whole affair was unfortunate.' Sara kept her tone cool. 'But if you managed to explain your chauvinistic behaviour satisfactorily to your child, then you can forget it. I assure you I already have.' She lifted her shoulders in a careless shrug. 'Besides, as kisses went, it was no big deal.'

His glower darkened, and she knew her jab had touched him in a soft spot.

'So,' she went on, 'if that's all—'

'It might have been no big deal to you,' he jeered, 'since you're used to being kissed by The Hottest Lips in Hollywood.'

'Yes.' She allowed an amused smile to play around

47

her mouth. 'I believe that *is* how Zach is currently billed.'

'How does it feel to be one in a long line of—'

'Of what?' Her eyes widened innocently.

'Trollops!'

'Oh, dear.' Laughter bubbled around her words. 'That *does* sound old-fashioned.'

'The word may be old-fashioned, but there's nothing old-fashioned about the kind of women Zach Grant hangs around with. Good lord, I sometimes wonder how the tabloids would manage to fill in page one if they had no pictures of Grant and some centrefold bimbo—'

She burst out laughing.

'What the hell's funny about that?'

'It's just…I can't believe you read the tabloids!'

'I don't read them,' he snapped. 'Andy does.'

'But you sneak a look…and you believe everything you see there. Right?'

'Where there's smoke, there's fire.'

'Not always.' Sara shook her head. 'Sometimes it's more a case of smoke and mirrors.' She took a sip from her mug, and remembered her manners. 'I've just made a pot of coffee. Would you like to come in and have a cup?'

She was sure he'd refuse; his attitude was so totally hostile.

To her astonishment he said, 'Thanks,' and walked past her…like a robot, granted—almost as if he wasn't responsible for his own response to her invitation.

Sara raised her brows, shut the door, and followed him through to the kitchen.

'So—' she took a blue and yellow stoneware mug

from the garish plastic tree on the counter '—your daughter has gone for a trip?'

'Yeah, with Chrissie Pratt and her parents.' Logan jammed his hands into his shorts pockets and prowled the kitchen restlessly. 'They're going to be gone for two days.'

'Cream and sugar?'

'Black, thanks.' He accepted the steaming mug.

She refilled her own and sat down at the table. 'How's the packing going?' she asked.

His glance was wary. 'What else did Andy tell you?'

Sara felt her nerves give a warning prickle. Had she wandered into forbidden territory? 'She just said you were packing her mother's stuff away in boxes.'

'Her mother's not around any more.'

'You have custody?'

Emotion flickered in his green eyes. It could have been pain. 'That's right.'

'Sole?'

'Yeah.'

It was pain; there was no mistaking it. Yes, forbidden territory; and, like an iceberg, only a small area was showing. 'It's a tough thing to face,' she said, 'the end of a marriage. But…you must have done something right—everything right—to end up with sole custody of your child.'

His laugh was hard. 'That's where you're mistaken,' he said. 'I did every damned thing wrong.'

'I don't see how you could—'

'Take my word for it.' His expression had become veiled, shutting her out. 'I did.'

He gulped down the rest of his coffee, thumped the mug on the table.

'I'll be off, then,' he said. 'Thanks for the java.'

'You're welcome.'

She saw him to the door.

He took a step away, and then turned.

'How about dinner tonight?' he asked abruptly. 'My place. Six-thirty.'

Sara's heart jumped. 'No, I think...better not.'

'I'd forgotten Andy was leaving...I've taken a couple of steaks out of the freezer; I was going to barbecue.'

'You can do one tonight, and the other tomorrow.' Her voice was steady, but her pulse was jagging up and down.

'Yeah, sure, I can do that. Forget it...it was just an idea...' He looked across at her for another moment longer, and then said, 'I'm off, then. Thanks again for the coffee.'

Logan spent the rest of the day gutting the attic. He finished around five o'clock. After a shower, he changed into a clean shirt and trousers, and went down to the kitchen to start preparing dinner.

Dinner for one, he mused wryly as he sipped from a glass of chilled dry Riesling.

He had just finished preparing a green salad to go with his steak, when he chanced to look out of the kitchen window...

At first he thought he must be seeing things, and he did a double-take. It was a mirage. No—he peered between the narrow slats of the venetian blinds—no mirage. Flesh and blood.

Wow!

She was wearing the dress she'd worn on the day of her arrival—the buttercup-yellow dress with the

nipped-in waist and the flirty skirt. Her feet were
adorned by strappy sandals whose high heels would have
pronged her to the lawn had she not tiptoed over it as
gingerly as if she were stepping on eggshells. Her hair
was swept up in a style that should have looked sophis-
ticated yet on the lovely Mrs Sara Wynter was sweetly
charming...

And in her hand she was swinging a bottle of wine.

This woman was not coming to borrow sugar!

Logan leaped into action. It took him less than sixty
seconds to rush to the patio table and add a second place
setting to the one already there; to add more greens and
sliced tomatoes to the salad; to snatch another wineglass
from the cabinet and set it beside his own.

By the time his guest was ascending the steps leading
to the front door, he was already halfway across the hall.

When she rang the bell, he swung the door open.

'Right on time.' With a wolfish smile, he caught her
wrist and drew her into the house. 'If there's one quality
I appreciate in a woman, it's punctuality.'

Sara sat slumped in an armchair in Logan's living
room—a room totally bare of knick-knacks, she'd already noticed—and took another sip of her wine. It was
a fine German Riesling. Her favourite. The man was
apparently a mind-reader; he'd had the bottle chilling in
the fridge.

She'd brought red, to go with the steak, though she
herself never drank red; it gave her a headache.

He'd accepted the offering and thanked her graciously, then just as graciously had ushered her into this
room with its comfortable sofas and Oriental rugs and
rosewood tables.

There they'd sat and talked, lightly, of this and that.

After about fifteen minutes, he'd excused himself, saying the barbecue coals should be ready about now, and he'd just throw on the steaks.

The moment she was alone, she'd slumped back in her seat. The strain of being bright, light and polite had left her completely drained.

He'd known she would come.

Despite her refusal, he'd been expecting her. She'd caught a glimpse of the patio as they'd passed the dining room's open door. The table was set for two.

She wasn't sure whether his assumption that she would end up accepting his invitation was a cause for irritation or amusement.

She decided to settle for both.

No, irritation was the more appropriate reaction. The more satisfying reaction. The man was arrogant, inconceivably arrogant. He took altogether far too much for granted.

'Penny for them.'

She hadn't heard him come back into the room. She straightened, and tilted her head up at him haughtily as he came to a halt in front of her.

'I was thinking,' she said, 'that you're very sure of yourself.'

'Yeah,' he grinned, 'pretty much so.'

He might be an over-confident jerk, but he was also irresistibly attractive. 'Tall, dark and handsome' didn't begin to do justice to the man. It left out his most devastating features: his sexual charisma, and his startling green eyes. Eyes that were fixed on her now, their clarity so very unsettling.

They didn't always have that clarity, though; sometimes they smoked over, like misty green glass.

When he'd kissed her yesterday, his eyes had smoked like that; and it had done strange things to her equilibrium…

Stop it! she told herself fiercely. Stop thinking about that kiss!

She dropped her gaze to his shoes.

He was wearing slip-ons, of fine charcoal-grey leather, perfectly polished and the same shade as his immaculately pressed trousers. His legs were long and muscular. She remembered how his thighs had felt, hard as granite, as he'd pressed them against her. Her throat felt dry; danger whispered a warning in her ears.

And she knew she shouldn't have come.

'Your husband—'

She jerked her head up so fast, she almost got whiplash.

'Yes? What about him?'

Logan dropped into an overstuffed armchair, lazily crossed his legs. 'Is he still in the picture?'

'Not in *my* picture. We're divorced.'

'Ah.' He nodded, his eyes never leaving hers.

She felt as if she was a fascinating specimen under a powerful microscope. She wriggled uncomfortably, wanting to change the subject, but before she could think of anything to say he spoke again.

'And how does Zach Grant fit into…your picture?'

Oh, lord, this was even worse. Zach had sworn her to silence about their true relationship—at least till after his present five-year contract with Sellarsby Studios expired, which it was due to in September.

She aimed for nonchalance. 'We're just good friends.'

'Now…that *does* have a familiar ring to it!'

'Doesn't it!'

'Were you…involved with him, while you were still married?'

'I've known Zach for years. I've been divorced for one week.' She shrugged. *Draw your own conclusions.* She didn't need to add that; she knew Logan Hunter would…and that he would come up with the wrong answer.

'So your divorce has just come through,' he murmured. '*Now* I understand why you sounded so "been there, done that!" when you said "It's a tough thing to face, the end of a marriage". It is, under any circumstances.'

To her dismay, she felt a smarting behind her eyes. It *had* been tough. But the failure of her marriage was not something she was about to discuss with Logan Hunter.

She'd only come up tonight for dinner because she'd felt sorry for him. She was not about to become involved in any heart-to-heart talks, about either her own failed marriage or his.

And she would do well to bear that in mind.

'Don't you think,' she said airily, rising to her feet, 'that we ought to check on the steaks? I did mention, didn't I, that I like mine rare?'

They lingered lazily over dinner, and afterwards reclined on cushioned loungers, sipping Drambuie from delicate Baccarat glasses. In comfortable silence, they watched the sun drift down, inch by spectacular inch, behind the forested hills.

When the final crimson rays had bled from the sky, stealthy shadows began to creep silently over the garden.

And on the heels of the shadows glided a light breeze that stirred the leaves…and brought Sara's perfume to him.

He'd noticed it earlier, and it had made him think of jasmine and roses…

Now it smelled more sultry, and it made him think of dark green woods and spicy glades. Long, hot kisses and sleek, tanned limbs. Arousing caresses and intimate explorations. It vibrated through his senses like a tsunami. And, dammit—he rubbed a hand over his eyes to erase a sudden vivid Technicolor vision of Sara Wynter naked in his arms—he was becoming aroused!

In the distance, thunder rumbled.

As if at a signal, Sara rose to her feet.

'Time to go back to the cottage,' she murmured. 'It's cooling off.'

Reluctantly, he stood. 'You're sure?' The timbre of his voice was husky. 'I could fetch you a jacket.'

She shook her head. 'No, thanks. It's getting late. But I've had a lovely evening…really enjoyed myself.'

'I can't persuade you…?'

'No.'

'I'll walk you back, then.'

'You don't have to.'

'I want to.'

'Oh. OK, then. Thanks.'

'Hang on a sec and I'll get a jacket.'

He ignored her protests and, striding inside, went through to the front hall. He stood for a moment by the closet, letting his ardour cool down. Then he slipped a suit jacket from its hanger and went back outside.

He draped the jacket over her shoulders, and as her perfume came to him again lust punched him in the gut with a ferocity that almost knocked his knees from under him.

It had been one hell of a mistake, he reflected grimly, to invite her for dinner. The thought of entertaining one of Zach Grant's women in the movie star's absence had, at the time, appealed to his sense of irony. But the passion that had erupted between them yesterday should have reminded him that there was danger involved in playing with fire.

One could go up in flames!

They walked together across the patio, and onto the lawn.

'Just a sec,' she murmured. 'I'm going to take off my sandals.'

She rested a hand on his shoulder as she slipped off the sandals and her breast brushed his arm. He raised his face to the heavens and prayed he'd be able to keep himself under control; that he wouldn't grab her and haul her against himself and kiss her till she begged for mercy.

The moon had appeared, round and pale, frail as tissue paper. The sky was a very dark purple...and now stars were appearing, one by one, as if minions were racing around the heavens, flicking on switches here, there and everywhere.

She lifted her hand from his shoulder.

'Thanks.' Her voice had a stiffness he hadn't noticed there a few moments ago.

They lapsed back into silence as they walked down the sloping lawn, but it wasn't a comfortable silence like those they'd somehow eased into over dinner. Tension tugged between them now—sexual tension—and Logan wondered if she'd sensed his arousal.

Woman's instinct. A powerful tool. And one a man should never underestimate.

He stifled a frustrated sigh. He'd give one of his eye-teeth, right now, to know what Sara Wynter was thinking.

She wanted him.

She'd been wanting him ever since he'd circled her wrist with his hand and drawn her into his house.

The touch of his fingertips on her skin had caused a conflagration of sizzling explosions that had rippled through her body to every erogenous zone she possessed.

And the aftershock still rippled through her now, making her giddy, elated, reckless.

Desperately she tried to cling to sanity. It was dangerous to feel this way. Terribly dangerous. Hadn't she sworn to herself that she'd keep her distance from this man?

She inhaled a deep breath and started to walk faster.

In two long strides, he'd caught up with her. He grabbed her hand. 'What's your hurry? How about a walk along to the end of the jetty before you go in?'

No way, she thought. No *way* would she stay outside in the moonlight with this man one moment longer than was necessary. She'd have to be crazy!

'OK,' she said. 'Why not?'

The jetty swayed under them as they stepped from the beach onto the wooden planks, and the tipsy floating motion only added to Sara's sense of unreality.

She drew in a deep breath of the salty air, savouring it; but the air itself was chilly and it was cutting through her thin dress. Grasping the lapels of the jacket draped over her shoulders, she pulled it more snugly around her, but as she did the lingering scent of its owner drifted up to her, and made her so giddy with longing, she almost stumbled.

When she and Logan reached the waist-high railing at the end of the jetty, he leaned back against it, and folded his arms across his wide chest.

'So, Mrs Sara Wynter...now that you're divorced, what are you going to do with the rest of your life?'

Sara stopped, and stood facing him, but making sure she stayed in her own space. The moon frosted his hair and she thought this was how he might look thirty years down the road—distinguished, and still incredibly attractive.

'Have you ever had plans—' she tried to see his eyes but they were shadowed '—that you didn't want to talk about in case just saying them out loud made them disappear?'

'No...but if there's even the remotest possibility that it might happen in this case I make haste to withdraw my question.' Amusement enriched his voice. 'I'd hate to be responsible for the death of your dreams. Granted, there are no bottles of bubble beads around, or soap bars, or—'

'Are you implying, Mr Hunter, that I have a temper?'

'I decline to answer on the grounds that I might incriminate myself—'

'Oh, all right!' Her lips twitched in a rueful smile. 'What I do—what I used to do, before my marriage—is design knitwear. One of a kind...mainly sweaters.'

'You were wearing one the other day—blue and silver, a very feminine creation…looked soft and feather-light.'

'Yes, that was one of my own designs. I knitted it myself…oh, it seems centuries ago now!'

The wind was rising and it tossed his hair around. He raked the strands back. 'I'm surprised you could stop designing. It was my impression that the urge to create isn't something that can be turned on and off at will.'

Sara moved over to the railing, grasped the top spar, and stared out over the jet and silver waves. She recalled how Travis had dismissed her work; the memory dulled her heart.

'Sometimes,' she said, 'the passion dies.'

'Ah.'

She sensed Logan watching her; his scrutiny made her uneasy. She took in a deep breath, and turned from the railing. 'I—'

'Perhaps,' he said quietly, 'the passion dies because it's been channelled in the…wrong…direction.'

'What do you mean?'

'You and…Zach Grant. I should imagine that, no matter what the circumstances, committing adultery must surely create a burden of guilt. Perhaps it was your guilt that caused you to lose your Muse—'

'And I should imagine,' Sara shot back hotly, 'that perhaps it was your sheer bloody arrogance that caused you to lose your wife!'

It was impossible to see his face, shadowed as it was in the moonlight, but his withdrawal from her—his emotional withdrawal—was unmistakable. She felt it as surely as she would have felt a slap on the mouth.

Remorse overwhelmed her. He had no way of knowing the true nature of her relationship with Zach Grant;

and she'd purposely allowed him to think the worst—
had been forced to, really, because of the unusual circumstances she found herself in. But her vicious thrust
at him had been totally uncalled for, and had obviously
jabbed him in the heart.

Oh, damn, why had she let her temper get the better
of her?

'Logan, I'm s—'

But he was obviously in no mood to accept an apology. With a rasping oath, he swept his jacket from her
shoulders and brushed past her. And as he strode off
along the jetty his leather soles hit the planks with such
force, she thought it a wonder he didn't go right through
the wood.

She was still standing, stunned, at the end of the dock,
when he reached his house, and slammed the front door.

Then, jolted by the reverberating sound...and more
than a little alarmed by the steadily rising wind...she
hurried back along the jetty to seek the shelter of
the cottage.

CHAPTER FIVE

LOGAN stretched, and yawned, and rolled back his swivel chair.

Scratching his hands vigorously through his hair, he glanced out of the study window as thunder crashed overhead.

It was some storm.

It had broken about an hour after he'd left Sara Wynter at the jetty. He'd been in the kitchen, emptying the dishwasher, when the first brilliant flash of lightning had slashed the heavens. Within minutes, the rain had started—torrential rain whirled against and around the house by a screeching, venomous gale.

Bethany had hated storms. She would have hated this night...

And she would have hated his leaving a woman alone in the dark, the way he'd left Sara Wynter.

He'd felt at the time that he had good reason to do so. But he could acknowledge now that it wasn't her wild and unfounded accusation that had made him walk out on her; it was his own feelings of guilt.

He sighed, his heart crushed by the heavy weight of his promise. The promise he hadn't fulfilled. It gnawed at him, relentlessly. He couldn't keep putting it off; he had to get to grips with it!

And surely there was no time like the present!

Throwing back his head, he closed his eyes and mentally printed out a heading:

SECOND WIFE.

And below the heading he wrote his mental checklist of attributes essential in a suitable bride.

LOOKS: plain, but not distractingly so.

HEIGHT: average.

BUILD: neatly assembled, but unobtrusively so.

VOICE: quiet.

MANNER: modest.

ATTITUDE: non-argumentative.

He drew a bold line under the word 'non-argumentative'.

Sara Wynter—he snorted—now *there* was an argumentative female, if ever there was one! Good lord, she'd been like a blonde Siamese cat, spitting at him that way on the jetty!

He smiled, a self-derisive twist of his lips. Why bother with a list? The woman he was looking for was, simply, the very opposite of Mrs Sara Wynter—

The phone shrilled, and he shot his chair forward.

Who the devil could that be? At this time of night?

Andy. Something had happened to Andy! His heart gave a giant lurch, and he grabbed the desk phone.

'Hunter!' he barked. 'Who—?'

'Logan.' Sara Wynter's voice shimmied along the line. 'I have a problem.'

'What?'

Thunder pealed overhead, and for a few moments all he could hear was a loud crackle, as if someone were frying bacon in his ear.

Then, 'Logan? Are you there?'

'Yeah, I'm here. So…what's your problem? You're afraid of thunder? Or is it the lightning that—?'

'No, dammit, I happen to love storms! But what's

bothering me is that this particular one has blown in the living-room window! The shutters are smashing around fit to waken the dead, and there's broken glass and rainwater everywhere. On top of that, there's a leak in the roof, just above my bed, and though I've hauled the shower curtain over it I was too late; the mattress is soaked, and the water's running all over the—'

'OK, I get the message.' Logan was already on his feet. 'Hang on. I'll be right down.'

Sara shivered as she opened the cottage door for Logan, and flinched as a blast of cold wind drove rain into the hall, further wetting her already damp jeans and sweatshirt.

'Look,' she said, 'I'm sorry I had to call you out this late, but I really had no option!'

His response was a noncommittal grunt.

He was carrying a heavy flashlight, and wearing a voluminous yellow slicker. On his feet was an enormous pair of rubber boots that made a reassuringly solid sound on the planked floor as he walked along the passage to the bedroom.

She stood behind him as he assessed the situation. The wind howled like a mad dog through the living room and flung sheets of rain through the jagged gaping maw where the windowpane had been. In the bedroom, water was now gushing through the hole in the roof in a veritable torrent, and the floor was awash.

'Disaster.' Logan's tone was brusque. 'Grab your stuff. You'll have to come up to the house with me.'

'But surely you can't just let it—'

He turned. 'Whoever buys the house is going to tear

this cottage down. Its only value is the land under your feet. Now…pack your bag and let's get out of here.'

She swallowed. 'All right. Er…will you get my toilet things out of the bathroom?'

'Sure.'

She packed as quickly as she could, and, throwing her anorak on, put up the hood and secured it tightly. When she went out into the passage, Logan was exiting the bathroom, holding her sponge bag. He stuffed it into a side pocket of her holdall.

'Right,' he said. 'Got everything?'

'I…think so,' she said breathlessly.

'Then let's go.'

The powerful gale, laden with salt spray and beach sand and tangled seaweed, whipped them up the slope like so much debris from the shore. By the time they reached the house, Sara felt as if the storm had taken her, personally, by the scruff of the neck and given her a thorough shaking!

When Logan had closed the front door against the full force of the wind, she dropped her bag on the carpet and slumped back exhaustedly against the nearest wall.

Gasping for breath, she watched Logan take off his slicker, shake it, and hang it in the hall closet. He was wearing a grey T-shirt and a pair of grey jogging bottoms. When he turned, she saw raindrops glistening in his black hair and streaming down his tanned face. He'd never looked more earthy, she thought…nor more starkly male…

He held out a hand for her anorak, and she saw his pecs ripple and bunch, and knew that if she were to touch them they would be iron-hard. She felt a spark of desire—

He snapped his fingers. 'Jacket!'

Good grief, he was talking to her the way he might talk to a dog! The spark died. With rising temper, she pushed herself from the wall, and ripped off the sodden anorak.

She shoved it at him.

'You have some nerve,' she snapped, 'to rent out a place with a leaky roof!'

Ignoring her attack as if it were the tantrum of a spoiled child, he hung her jacket in the closet.

'You can use the guest room,' he said, and, scooping up her travel bag, strode off across the hall.

Sara glared after him for a full ten seconds, and only when he disappeared through a side doorway did she jerk herself into action and hurry after him.

The guest room turned out to be on the main floor, but cut off from it by a swing door and isolated from the rest of the house by a long narrow hallway.

It faced north and might have been a 'cold' room but for the pink-painted walls and the soft green fabric of the bedspread, drapes and carpet. The furniture was rosewood, with elegant lines and a satin-smooth patina.

Logan ushered her forward. 'Don't worry that the bed might be damp—I have a caretaker coming in on a regular basis to air everything out.' He looked around and frowned. 'It is a bit *chilly* in here, though. He turns the heating off at the end of June. You sure you'll be all right?'

'Of course.' She moved over to the window and drew the folds of the curtains together, to shut out the sounds of the storm. The velvet fabric was luxuriously heavy, and hung in soft folds to the plush green carpet.

'Would you like something to warm you up?' he asked tersely as she turned to him again. 'Tea? Cocoa?'

She shook her head. 'No, a hot shower will do the trick.' She tried to smile, but her lips felt frozen.

He nodded towards a door to her left. '*En-suite* bathroom—you should find everything you need in there.'

'Thank you.' The words came out stiffly.

'Yeah.' He strode back towards the door.

It was on the tip of her tongue to call, 'Wait!' She really hated fighting, and she was the one who had started it. But before she could speak he was outside the room and closing the door behind him.

With a regretful sigh she unzipped her bag and draped her robe over the bed. Then, taking her toilet things and her nightie, she went into the bathroom, where she peeled off her clothes and stepped into a steaming shower.

Dammit, Logan thought as he crossed his bedroom, the guest room had been *cold*...and he'd seen her actually shivering.

After her shower, she'd probably chill down again as soon as she got into bed. How could he possibly go to sleep himself, knowing she was going to lie chittering all night?

He'd started to take off his T-shirt; now he tugged it on again over his jogging bottoms, and strode out of the room. Downstairs, he veered into the living room where he made for the logbox. After gathering up logs and kindlers, along with newspaper and matches, he set off for the guest room.

While she was in the bathroom he'd get a fire going in the hearth. Women took forever to titivate before going to bed; she'd be in there for an age, brushing her hair, her teeth, creaming her skin, doing whatever females did before they finally bedded down for the night. She'd be pleasantly surprised, when she came out, to find the chill gone from the air, and a cheery fire going in the hearth.

Sara yawned as she stepped out of the shower. She'd only stayed under the hot spray for a few minutes, but it had drained her of the last remnants of her energy. She was tired and she couldn't wait to collapse into bed.

Yawning again, she towelled herself dry, and slipped into her red silk shortie nightie. She swept her brush through her hair, brushed her teeth in record time, applied a blob of cream to her hands, and opened the bathroom door.

She'd left only one light on before going for her shower—a bedside lamp, with a low-wattage bulb and a pink shade that made the room glow. Now, as she stepped into the bedroom, she saw shadows flickering on the walls, heard an odd crackling sound, smelled the scent of resin.

Someone stepped forward from the shadows and she gasped.

'Logan!' Her heart gave a grinding bump, and she pressed a hand over it. 'What are you doing here?'

Logan asked himself the same question!

'Sorry.' He almost choked as he spoke. 'I thought I'd be gone before you came out, but—'

'You didn't have to light a—'

'No problem.' He should move. He told his legs to

move, to get going, for Pete's sake, but they stubbornly refused to obey. He swallowed. He gawked. He knew he shouldn't, but that slinky red thing she was wearing... Lust roared up inside him like a tiger on the loose.

Down, boy!

He cleared his throat. 'I...um...thought you'd be cold.' He shrugged. 'I pictured you...'

Not like this! He'd pictured her chittering in bed, curled up with her arms around her knees and her skin ridged with giant goosebumps—

'What?' She raised her hands in a nervous gesture, and the movement caused the nightie to slither up her body...and, with an almost imperceptible crackle, cling there.

'Static!' Blushing furiously, she tugged the hem back to its original position, skimming the top of her thighs. 'There, decent again.'

She scurried over to the bed to get her robe, which was lying on the spread.

Decent? Logan somehow managed to stifle an anguished groan. She called that decent? And look at her *now*! She was leaning over the bed—her frantic embarrassment obviously blinding her to the blatant provocation of her posture—and the reaching position had sucked up her nightie again. He was exposed to a mindboggling view of endlessly long legs topped by a sexy little butt wrapped in red silk that stuck to the perfectly formed curves like cling film.

He closed his eyes, feeling like a peeping Tom. He tried to erase the images of her centrefold body. Too late. They were now—front, rear and side—printed indelibly on his retinae in glorious 3D Technicolor.

'Oh, drat!' she muttered.

He opened his eyes…and then mentally rolled them as he saw she still wasn't 'decent'. She was having a problem putting on the robe. The sleeves were inside out. She was all tangled up, and getting worse by the second.

'Here.' He was, after all, a gentleman. 'Let me…'

'Oh, I can do it,' she said in a rush. He heard the panic in her voice, and she fumbled quickly with the robe as he approached. Fumbled, and dropped it.

'Oh, lord…' She bent to retrieve it.

He stooped too.

Their heads bumped together.

His was harder.

She winced, and, grasping her by the shoulders, he straightened, pulling her up with him.

'Are you OK?' he asked.

'Yes.' Her voice was a bit shaky. 'Just a little…dizzy…'

Still off balance, she tilted forward and her breasts brushed his chest. He drew in a sharp breath, and tightened his grip.

A sound, close to a whimper, came from her throat.

He heard it and the tiger roared again.

He slid his hands down her back, and clasped his arms around her waist in a loose but inescapable embrace. His thumb knuckles rested on her spine. She looked up at him, her beautiful turquoise eyes dazed. She seemed so innocent, so young, so…fresh.

Was this how she looked when she was about to have sex with Zach Grant?

The black thought slammed against his ribs with the shattering power of a runaway train. Until this moment, he'd never actually pictured the two of them together, in

that way. Now the image exploded in his mind with a
lurid vividness that had the lust tiger roaring in anger
and outrage, before slinking away into the forest.

Logan drew in a deep breath, dropped his arms, and
stepped back.

'Sorry,' he said stiffly. 'That shouldn't have happened.' He somehow managed to fake a wry smile.
'Even Andy has hauled me over the coals for my Dark
Ages approach to women. So—' he cleared his throat
'—I'll let you get off to bed. Feel free to stoke up the
fire…I've dumped enough logs there on the hearth to
see you through the night. Then in the morning—' he
turned and made for the door '—I'll get on the phone
and find you a nice chalet where you can finish your
holiday in peace.'

She didn't protest. And why should she? She must be
as eager to get out of this house as he was to have her
gone. His hand was on the doorknob when she spoke.

'Logan?' Her voice was husky.

What now? He turned.

Her face was very pale.

'I just wanted you to know I'm sorry too…for what
I said on the jetty. Implying that the split-up between
you and your wife was probably your fault. I was way
out of line, and—'

'No,' he said harshly. 'You were right. I *was* responsible, but not in the way you imagine.' He turned the
knob and opened the door. Had she heard the anguish
in his voice? Did she, dammit, see the pain in his eyes?
'My wife and I are not divorced, Mrs Wynter. My wife
is dead.'

The storm had exhausted its frenzy by morning, and
when Sara got up at seven-thirty and drew back the

green velvet curtains the brightness of the sunshine dazzled her eyes.

The brilliance did nothing, however, to lift her spirits. What Logan had told her still hung heavily on her mind. How cruel her accusation had been. How thoughtlessly shot out. Her heart ached with regret. She sighed as she turned from the window. His wife was dead. And that must be why he was selling the property. Memories would abound. Memories that had the power to hurt.

And she had hurt him further.

She had to get out of here; she couldn't bear the tension that existed between them.

Unable to shake off her depression, she stripped the bed, showered, and got dressed in a yellow T-shirt, jeans and sneakers. She applied no make-up, scraped her hair back in a no-nonsense ponytail, and then rummaged in her bag for her address book.

She thumbed through it till she found the phone number Zach had given her, along with his hotel room number.

There was a phone on the bedside table, and she made the long-distance call.

'I'm sorry,' said the desk clerk, 'Mr Grant is in the pool.'

'I'd like to leave a message,' Sara said. 'Please ask him to call me back on this number as soon as possible...'

After she'd hung up, she bundled the bedlinen under her arm and made for the kitchen.

There was no sign of Logan. But he was up. The coffee was made, and a packet of bagels was sitting by the toaster.

She went out into the hall and wandered around, in search of a laundry room.

She opened a couple of doors, with no success, and had just opened a third, realised it was a study, and was about to close the door again, when the phone on the desk rang.

She hesitated. It could be Zach. She waited for Logan to pick up an extension somewhere else in the house, but when he didn't, after three rings, she scooted across the room and scooped up the handset.

'Hello?' Her voice came out breathlessly.

'Honey, it's Zach—'

'Oh, thank goodness! Listen, we've had an awful storm here—'

'We had it too,' came the amused response. 'It was a dilly!'

'Zach, can you send somebody to come and get me? The cottage is a disaster...I'm up at the house. Mr Hunter let me stay here last night. But...well, I feel I'm imposing.'

'Honey, of course. I'll zip over myself. But it won't be till this evening. We're going to be shooting till around four. OK?'

Sara suppressed a murmur of disappointment. She wanted to leave, and leave now. But she had no choice but to wait. 'That's fine, Zach. I'll be looking out for you.'

'Take care,' he said. 'Now I've got to rush. See you this evening.'

Sara hung up, and turned to leave the room.

And that was when she saw the portrait.

It was gold-framed, and enormous, and it hung above

the marble fireplace. It was startling in its impact, and for a moment Sara stood frozen.

Logan's wife.

It had to be.

Feeling oddly shaky, she put a hand on the desk to support herself. It was the most disturbing sensation, to have those huge brown eyes looking straight at her. Keenly. Thoughtfully. As if the woman was wondering exactly what this stranger, this unknown female, was doing in her house.

Sara shivered. She wanted to look away, but couldn't. The portrait had her in its thrall.

What an exquisitely beautiful woman. Her face was a perfect oval, her features patrician, her chestnut hair rich and wavy, and upswept in an immaculate coil. The word 'elegant', Sara reflected, could have been coined for Logan Hunter's late wife. There was elegance in the tilt of her head, in the curve of her throat, in the pose of the slender hands on her lap, with their shell-pink polish.

Her wedding ring was gold, her engagement ring crusted with diamonds. They sparkled, just as the eyes did, but, whereas the sparkle of the gems was cold, the sparkle in the eyes was warm—

A small sound from behind startled her.

Turning, her eyes wide, she saw Logan standing in the open doorway. Her heart lurched off in an erratic race.

His eyes were dark, his expression grim. He looked from her to the portrait, and back to her again.

'What the *hell*,' he asked, 'are you doing in here?'

CHAPTER SIX

SARA had the uncomfortable feeling she had been caught doing something sneaky. But she hadn't, not really.

'I was looking for the laundry room—'

'Oh, yeah.' He leaned a shoulder against the door-frame and regarded her coolly. 'This certainly looks like a laundry room. So what are you waiting for? Go ahead. Stuff the bedlinen into...let me see...that filing cabinet, add water, and a sprinkle of detergent—'

'You really are a sarcastic beast.' All feeling of discomfort gone, Sara allowed her temper free rein. 'Just let me finish what I was going to say. I was opening doors, looking for a laundry room, and when the phone rang—'

'Ah. You took it upon yourself to answer it—'

'Because I was expecting a call.'

'From Zach Grant.' His tone was devoid of emotion.

'As a matter of fact...yes.'

'And how did he know you were here?'

'I phoned him when I got up. He was returning my call.'

'Ah.'

'I asked him to come and pick me up.'

'And is he going to oblige?'

'Yes.' Sara gripped her bundle of washing more tightly. 'But not till this evening, I'm afraid.'

'So we're stuck with each other till then.' He pushed

himself from the door. 'The washer and dryer are in the kitchen,' he said over his shoulder. 'Behind the louvred doors.'

She trotted after him like a puppy who had been disobedient—but all she had done was look at the portrait of his wife. Surely that was no crime!

'What do you want for breakfast?' he asked curtly as she tugged back the louvred doors.

'I'll just have coffee, thanks.'

She dropped the bedlinen into the washing machine, along with a scoop of detergent, and set the machine going.

When she turned he was pouring two mugs of coffee.

'I'm sorry,' she said, 'if you felt my going into your study was...an intrusion.'

He made a humph sound which she wasn't sure how to interpret.

'I really didn't mean to upset you—'

'Would you like bacon and eggs? Cereal? Juice is in the fridge; help yourself—'

'No, thank you. As I said, I'll just have coffee.' Anger burning her cheeks, she crossed to the table and picked up one of the steaming mugs. 'I wouldn't want to make myself more of a nuisance than I already am.'

She knew that if she didn't get out of there, right now, she'd start throwing things.

She stalked out of the kitchen and along to the front door. Once outside she hesitated only briefly, before deciding to go down to the jetty.

She was almost there when she heard Logan shouting from behind, 'Hang on a minute!'

She turned, to see him coming down the front steps.

'Wait up!' he called.

She kept walking.

She was halfway along the jetty before he got to her. He kept pace with her as she continued walking.

He said, 'I was thinking—'

'Well, what a pleasant change!'

'—that under the circumstances there's no reason why we can't behave in a civilised manner.'

'You wouldn't know civilised, Mr Hunter, if it jumped up and punched you on the nose!'

They had reached the end of the jetty. Sara leaned back stiffly against the railing and he stood facing her, their positions of the previous evening reversed.

'You are rude,' she said coldly, 'you are obnoxious, and, to top it all, you are utterly—'

'Charming.' He grinned. And he was.

His green eyes twinkled wickedly down at her...and she melted. For the life of her, she couldn't remember what final annihilating insult she'd been about to fling at him.

But she did remember how brusquely he'd treated her...and she did have some pride.

'Regardless of how charming *you* may think you are, *I* still think an apology would be appropriate!'

From his shirt pocket he whisked a white daisy which he must have plucked from the lawn as he'd chased after her. And before she could even decide whether or not to accept it he threaded it into her hair, above her left ear.

'There.' He stepped back to admire his handiwork. 'Apology accepted?'

When Travis had been particularly cold to her, he would on rare occasions apologise. His apology would take the form of hothouse roses, perfect, scarlet, exorbitantly expensive. Not once had she felt moved by those offerings, the way she was now by Logan's simple gesture.

She reached up, touched the daisy as if to reassure herself that it was really there. He was waiting, eyes fixed on her, for her response. Her throat ached a little, and when she spoke her voice came out huskily.

'Thank you,' she said. 'Apology accepted.'

'Good.' He was still looking at her, and odd little tingles started to dance along her skin, and inside her skin, to places deep down inside her.

Dangerous.

'So.' She turned away and looked out over the water. 'What are your plans for today?' All the world could have disappeared; she was aware of nothing but the man moving to stand beside her.

'I was going to go for a sail.' He leaned a lazy hip against the railing. 'Fancy coming along?'

She found herself looking at him again and tried not to notice how the sun shimmered highlights in his black hair. 'You have a boat? Well, of course you must have a boat; how else would you get here? But where is it?'

'Boathouse, over there—' he gestured with one hand '— hidden by those trees. So…are we on, or not?'

'Well…'

'Well? Is that a yes or a no?'

'I don't know. You've taken me by surprise.' She gnawed her lip. 'I'd have to be back in time for—'

'Loverboy.' He shrugged. 'No problem.'

Sara flinched. *Loverboy.* She could, of course, put a stop to the charade she'd been playing. With a few words, she could change Logan's opinion of her, could set out to enjoy this one day, in the company of a man who was, by her own private acknowledgement, charming!

She debated with herself for a long moment, and then she sighed.

'I have to tell you something,' she said quietly.

'Yeah?'

'Zach Grant isn't my lover.'

She saw his expression change, saw the twinkle of amusement disappear. But he made no response, just waited for her to go on.

'I told you the truth when I said I've known him for years. But we've never had any kind of a... thing...going. I'm sorry I let you labour under the delusion that we did. It's just not true. The two of us have a strictly platonic relationship. It's always been that way, and always will be.'

She desperately wanted to explain the *whole* situation to him, but of course she wasn't free to do so; it wasn't her secret to share.

He didn't answer. He was frowning, his gaze dubious.

'Logan—' she touched his arm '—please believe me.'

'Damned if I don't,' he said slowly. And his grin came back, inching over his face and twinkling in his eyes. 'Damned if I don't, Mrs Sara Wynter.' He grasped her hand in his, and swung it.

'So what are we waiting for?' he said, leading her back along the jetty. 'Let's get this show on the road. We'll pack a lunch. I have something special I'd like to show you.'

The 'something special' turned out to be a lovely crescent of beach on the western, uninhabited side of the island. Tucked in a fold between two high cliffs, and accessible only by boat, it was both sheltered and private.

The water was shallow there, and not too cold. On their arrival, they had a brisk swim, and then Logan tossed her a Frisbee and they fooled around for a while, before eating lunch.

During the meal, they talked. And talked. And talked.

Afterwards, they moved their towels under the shade of an enormous alder tree. There they lay and relaxed, side by side, she in her crocheted white bikini and he in his black trunks…and talked some more.

He was easy company. And unlike Travis, who always centred conversation on himself, Logan appeared truly interested in her and her designing.

She found herself opening up. Telling him things about herself she'd never told anyone else.

Looking up at the pieces of blue sky visible through the leafy green branches, she heard herself saying dreamily, 'What I'm planning to do when I go home is set up my own boutique, where I'll sell only Sally Cole creations.'

'Sally Cole? That's the name of your line?'

'Mmm.'

'You're aware that if you venture out on your own your life won't *be* your own? At least for the first few years. It'll have to be all work and no play. Competition's tough these days, Sara—tougher than it's ever been.'

She rolled over onto her side, and, supporting herself on her elbow, glared at him. 'I'm not afraid of hard work!'

'Whoa! I wasn't attacking. I was only pointing out

that if you're to succeed you'll have to put your whole heart into it.'

'Well, that's a given! It applies to any area where we want to succeed…not only business, but sports, studies, relationships…'

'Yeah.' His gaze narrowed. 'And marriage.'

She sensed he was thinking of her failed marriage. Not only thinking about it, but casting blame. It rankled.

She hated to be put on the defensive, but that was exactly where she was right now. Anger prickled her nerves. And, despite her attempts to stay cool, she felt her temper rise.

Scrambling to her feet, she looked down at him belligerently.

'I did put my heart into my marriage! I did everything in my power to make it work.'

He got up too.

She stepped back. But found herself up against the trunk of the alder tree.

He extended a hand and she could almost see the olive branch in it. 'Whoa,' he said again, the soft way he might have spoken to a nervous filly. 'Don't get your dander up! Regardless of what you might think, I wasn't criticising—'

'Yes, you were. Obliquely, maybe, but you were. Criticising me because my marriage was a failure. Just because you were lucky enough to have a perfect marriage—'

He grabbed her wrist, sharply. His green eyes were pained. 'Don't do this, Sara. Please. If I was lucky, I've paid the price.'

Her anger vanished in a flash as she met his gaze, heard the anguish in his voice. Her shoulders slumped, and she buried her face in her hands. 'I'm sorry.' The words were muffled through her fingers. 'Oh, I'm so sorry...'

He tugged her hands from her face, tilted up her chin, made her look at him.

'It's all right,' he said quietly. 'No harm done. We all have our own demons to conquer. Come back, sit down. We'll have to leave soon...but we have a little while yet.'

Still teary, she let him lead her back to her towel. She sat down and, tucking her legs up, looped her arms around her knees. She looked out over the bay, her vision blurred. She was vaguely aware that Logan had sat down beside her.

She took in a shaky breath.

'My divorce,' she said in a low voice, 'was ugly. And I really don't want to talk about it. But although I wasn't to blame for the failure of our marriage I *am* to blame for marrying Travis in the first place. I never should have.'

'Why did you?'

She shrugged. 'I was only nineteen when I met him, and my head was filled with romantic dreams. You know the kind of stuff—looking for Mr Right, the Only Man for Me. It's garbage. People should marry because they have the same values, and because they like each other—'

'And what about love?'

'Love blinds people to reality. And who knows what love is, anyway? It means different things to different people. And in its name men and women hurl themselves into a lifetime of living together. It's crazy! Now, *arranged* marriages—there's a concept I can relate to:

unions that aren't based on airy-fairy notions but on substance. Romance is for the birds.'

'So…when you marry again, you'll go into it with your eyes wide open.'

'Good lord, no!' She shook her head vehemently. 'I'll never marry again! Never!'

Logan took her left hand and ran a fingertip lightly over the pale mark where her rings had been. 'This finger is destined to remain forever bare, then?'

'Forever bare.'

'You really have the most beautiful hands,' he murmured.

She stared at the hand lying resting over his broad palm. Her skin was smooth and lightly tanned, the fingers slender, the nails oval and unpainted. Beautiful? She'd never have labelled them that herself. But she had to admit that they did look feminine, delicate, in comparison with his strong male hand, with its long, capable fingers.

She wondered what they would feel like, those slightly calloused hands, caressing her naked skin—

'An artist's hands.' He raised her fingers to his lips and, turning them over, pressed a lingering kiss to her palm.

Shock trembled through her. She became intensely aware of the tangy ocean scent on his skin, and the musky scent of his hair.

'So, Mrs Sara Wynter—' he raised his head, and his lips were mere inches from hers '—you're nobody's woman.'

'I'm my *own* woman.'

He smiled, and the warmth of it set her pulses off in a lilting dance. 'For the moment…'

'For ever...' But the protest came out weakly.

'You and I,' he said, 'have some unfinished business.'

'We...have?'

'That kiss...' his lips glided a path over her shoulder '...the one by the waterfall...'

'What about it?' She sounded as if she was having trouble breathing.

'I've never been one—' he touched his lips lightly to the sensitive skin below her ear '—to leave things half done.'

She swayed towards him.

He plunged his hands into her hair, holding great bunches of it; it looked so heavy, so thick, but it felt as insubstantial as moonbeams. He used it as ropes, to pull her face to his. And all the while he was drowning in the depths of her glorious, long-lashed eyes. 'I like—' he teased her lips with his and drew back again '—to finish what I start.'

Her skin was perfumed by the lotion she'd smoothed on after her swim; it was spicy and tantalising, and it roused the tiger of lust that had been drowsing within him.

'I don't know,' she whispered, 'if that would be a good idea...in this case...'

'Oh, yes—' he kissed her eyelids '—it would be a very good idea. We're both adults, neither of us is spoken for, so what's the harm?'

None. None that she could think of. And then she stopped even trying to think as he claimed her lips with a self-assurance that jellied her resistance and seared her blood.

He kissed her, and kissed her some more, till she thought she would pass out for lack of air; when finally he slid his mouth away, they were no longer sitting, but sprawled back, half across her towel, half across the sand.

But even as she tried to regain an upright position Logan tumbled her down again. And somehow he was now on his back, and she was on top. And he was grinning up at her.

Her tousled hair swung forward, brushing his cheeks.

His arms were around her waist, clamping her to him in a way that was terrifyingly intimate. And fraught with danger.

'Let me go!'

'Uh-uh!' He chuckled.

She dared not kick. Such a movement would have caused her thighs to jerk against who knew what. Her hands—which, thank heaven, were free—were her only tool.

She grabbed his hair and held fast. 'Let me up,' she panted, 'or I'll pull!'

He laughed.

So she pulled.

He grimaced. 'Ouch!' he protested. But she could tell, by the mocking gleam in his eyes, that he was in no pain.

'Tell you what,' he drawled. 'Kiss me, once, and I'll let you go.'

She fixed him with a disbelieving stare. 'Oh, sure!'

'Scout's honour.'

'Hmm.' She caught the tip of her tongue between her teeth. Could he be trusted? 'Just one kiss?'

'Just one kiss. From you to me.'

Just one kiss. No harm in that, surely. And it *was* a tempting proposition. She dropped her gaze to his mouth. He really had the most wonderful lips. They were beautifully shaped, and smooth, the lower lip a shade fuller than the upper. Right now, they were slightly parted, and looked moist and inviting and—

She kissed him.

His arms tightened convulsively around her.

He tasted of sea and musk and magic. Deep inside her, in response, muscles clenched, nerves tingled, blood hummed.

She felt her breasts swell, the peaks tighten—and she hastened to assure herself that the tell-tale signs would be too subtle for Logan to notice. But even as she did she was suddenly made startlingly aware of his own unmistakable arousal…and she thought her heart would stop.

Her breath caught in a gasp as he chose that moment to overturn her. He supported himself with his hands flat on the sand, at either side of her head. His face was flushed, his eyes hazy with passion.

'Sara Wynter—' his voice was thick '—you know what I want. And I think you want it too, just as badly as I do…'

Her answer was a faint whimper.

'I thought so.' He moved his body ever so slightly, and she moaned. He was driving her crazy, tempting, teasing, prolonging…

'So,' he said roughly, 'you'll forgive me, if I do what I have to do…'

Sara's pulses gave a wild lurch and she closed her eyes. He wouldn't need forgiving. She wanted him, more than she'd ever wanted anything in her life. She felt as if she was hovering on a brink—delirious pleasure on one side, bitter regrets on the other. Which way would she fall? Oh, she was leaning, leaning towards that deliriously seductive pleasure—

He leaped to his feet.

She opened her eyes, gaped up at him.

The sun was at his back, his face was shadowed. But she could see the flash of white teeth as he slanted his lips in a self-deprecatory grin.

'No cold showers here; I guess we're going to have to make do with the ocean.'

And even as she reeled in confusion he leaned over, swept her up in his arms and raced towards the water.

He plunged out till he was waist-deep. Sara finally got her act together, gathered her breath, and opened her mouth to give vent to a protesting scream.

But before she could make a sound he dropped her like a stone. And the last thing she heard, just before she went under, was her tormentor's wicked rumble of laughter.

CHAPTER SEVEN

LOGAN was the first to spot the sleek white cabin cruiser skimming towards the jetty that evening. He'd gone inside to get Sara's luggage, and he'd just come back and deposited it at the top of the verandah steps when she heard him say, 'Zach's coming.'

She got up from the lounger where she'd been relaxing since dinner. This was it, then. She stifled a sound of regret as she crossed to join Logan, who was now leaning against the railing, looking out over the water.

'Have you been wondering,' he asked, without taking his gaze from the fast-approaching cruiser, 'why I didn't...press my advantage this afternoon?'

Sara's cheeks became hot. 'Of course not!'

He turned to look at her, and she knew by his raised brows that her fiery blush told quite a different story.

'You *have* been wondering,' he said quietly, 'why I threw us both into the ocean instead of—'

'You did say "Just one kiss"!'

'Sara...' Logan's eyes had darkened '...putting a stop to what was happening between us on the beach...it was one of the hardest things I've ever had to do. But we're both adults, and the truth of the matter is I was unprepared.'

She heard the embarrassment in his voice, and it touched her. When she responded, her own voice was husky.

'You don't have to explain yourself to me, Logan. I

agree. If we'd...had sex...it would have been totally irresponsible.' And then, from somewhere deep inside her and without her conscious consent, came the shaky confession, 'It's been...two years since I've...you know. And I'm not on the pill—I get these side effects. So...'

'It's been five years for me. Since Bethany died.'

She knew it wasn't easy for a man to talk about such things, and his raw honesty brought the sting of tears.

'Logan—'

'Ahoy, up there!'

Zach's shout from the boat shattered the moment.

Sara waved in response, but neither she nor Logan took their eyes from each other.

'Well,' she said awkwardly, 'if you'll help me carry down my things, I'll be on my—'

'Stay.'

She stared. *'Stay?'*

'Yes. Why not? You've refused to take me up on my offer of a chalet in lieu of the cottage...and I feel I've done you out of the rest of your vacation. I want you to stay!' He smiled, a coaxing smile.

'Logan,' she protested weakly, 'you know that's not feasible...the way we—'

'Yeah, I know what you mean. But Andy'll be back tomorrow...we'll have a chaperon.'

'That's tomorrow! What about *tonight*?'

'I've a lot of paperwork to catch up on. I've been intending to get to it this evening...I'll keep myself busy, keep myself out of mischief! Come on, Sara. I've been feeling pretty damned guilty about the poor welcome I gave you the day you arrived...let me make up for it!'

Sara chewed on her lower lip. 'I don't know how Zach would take it, after coming all this way to pick me up...'

'Hell, if he's the friend you say he is, he'll be pleased you're having a good time! You are, aren't you?'

She screwed up her nose. 'Are you *sure* you want me to stay?'

'Absolutely.'

'OK. I'll go and talk with Zach—'

'Great! Oh, dammit, there's the phone. Look, bring the guy up. The least we can do is offer him a drink or something, before we send him on his way.' He grinned, and Sara had the oddest sensation that her heart was tilting.

'Right,' she said. 'Will do.'

Logan strode off to get the phone, and she set off to tell Zach he'd be returning to Vancouver alone.

'Sara?' Logan called out her name as he came out of his study. His voice echoed back in the empty foyer.

And was met by silence.

How long had he been on the phone? Ten minutes? And still Sara hadn't come back—with or without Zach.

He went into the living room and crossed to the bay window.

The white cabin cruiser bobbed gently at the jetty. But there was no sign of anyone walking up from the—

Ah, they were both on the boat.

He could see them, but his vision was obscured by the heat haze shimmering up off the beach. They were embracing. And they appeared to be glued together in a position that by no limitation of the imagination could be termed merely 'friendly'!

It was an illusion. It *had* to be.

Logan leaned forward, cupped a hand over his eyes in an attempt to cut out the glare. It didn't help.

Muttering under his breath, he moved behind the telescope, and squinted through the eye-piece.

They were kissing!

Outrage thundered through him—outrage and fury.

Zach Grant had Sara's face framed in his tanned hands, her long blonde hair was tousled around his wrists and she—*she* was doing the pelvic tilt against his lower torso with all the finesse and abandon of a street-walker!

Half-blinded by rage at the way she'd fooled him, he was out of the house in less time than it took to shake a rat's tail. Down the steps and the lawn, across the beach and onto the jetty.

And not until his feet were pounding solidly and heavily and noisily against the wooden planks did the couple even begin to unravel themselves from each other.

'*Platonic?*' he shouted as he ran, startling a nearby seagull into flapping up from the water and taking off with an indignant scream. 'You call this *platonic*?'

He skidded to a halt alongside the boat and glared down at the couple, who were just beginning to turn and look up at him. 'You are one cheap little bitch!' Along with the insult, he shot invisible contempt-tipped arrows into the wide turquoise eyes gazing up incredulously at him. 'Two years since you've had sex? Huh! Tell *that* to the Marines! I hope you didn't tell loverboy that you're staying on here with me. No way! No bloody way! You lying, conniving—'

'Logan.'

He heard her voice. He kept going. 'You and your sleazy fancy boy can just turn around and get out—'

'Logan.'

He heard her voice again. It sounded thready and weak. He realised that the woman in the boat was staring up at him as if he were something escaped from a zoo, and at exactly the same moment, with a jolt of shock, he noticed she was wearing pink. Sara had been wearing yellow. His mind boggled in bewilderment.

A finger poked him. In the back. Hard.

'Logan.'

He closed his eyes. His heart sank to his toes and beyond, down through the jetty to the ocean floor.

With a shuddering inhalation, he turned. Slowly turned. Dreading to see what he knew he would see.

Sara.

She was standing behind him.

Her face was pale.

'B-but…' he stuttered. He jerked his head round and looked at the woman in the boat. Was he going out of his mind? Was he seeing double? Did she have a twin?

He turned back to Sara.

'This is my mother, Logan.' Her voice was as flat as the expression in her eyes. 'She's Zach's personal secretary. I had no idea she'd be coming with him. Mom hates the water, she almost drowned once, when she was a child. But Zach was worried about me when I phoned. He thought I sounded…' her mouth twisted in a travesty of a smile '…not quite myself.'

'But…where were you…just now?'

'Over at the cottage, returning a book Zach borrowed last time he was here.'

Logan felt the jetty tremble as Zach Grant bounded up from the boat. Then it trembled again as he pulled Sara's mother up beside him. He put an arm around her.

Sara walked past Logan, and took up a stance beside her mother.

Now that they were close together, Logan could see the differences between them. Sara's hair was a shade lighter than her mother's, and her mother had fine lines around her mouth and her eyes. Though their figures were similar, Sara was slightly taller, her mother's waist not quite so slender. Their eyes were the same glowing turquoise, though the older woman's now were hard with anger.

'Mr Hunter,' she said, 'I'm Paula Kincaid. I don't know what's been going on here, but it seems to me you owe my daughter an apology.'

'Sara—I'm so sorry. You and your mother...you look so alike. I thought—'

'You thought I was kissing Zach. Even after all the talking we did, after the way I...opened up to you, you thought that.' The coldness in her voice hit him like a punch in the gut. 'You thought I was a liar—'

'Sara, please—'

'I don't want to hear it, Logan. And I have nothing more to say to you. Ever. I need to get my things.'

'Sara—'

She ignored Logan and turned to Zach. 'Will you come and help me, Zach? Mom, we'll be right back.'

She and Zach turned and made their way along the jetty. Logan was determined to go after them, to talk with Sara.

'Excuse me,' he muttered, 'I'm going to—'

'No.' Paula Kincaid stepped in front of him. 'My daughter has gone through enough, without getting involved with the likes of you, Mr Hunter. Let her be.'

She was right. He'd destroyed Sara's trust. And what

the hell had driven him to act the way he had? Why had
he been so furious at the sight of her in Zach Grant's
arms? Had it just been rage because she'd made a fool
of him? Or had it been jealousy because he'd wanted
the alluringly lovely blonde to be in his own arms...?

'You seem to have been under the impression that
Zach and Sara were having an affair.' Paula Kincaid's
voice broke into his tangled thoughts. 'Zach and I are
married, Mr Hunter, and have been for the past two
years.'

'Married?'

'Married,' she repeated firmly. 'But I'd appreciate it
if you'd keep the information to yourself. Zach's present
five-year contract calls for him to present a ''swinging
bachelor'' image—just as all his previous contracts have
done—and until this one runs out in early September we
have to keep our relationship strictly under wraps.'

'Don't worry.' Logan felt groggy, and wondered if
he'd ever manage to think straight again. Shoving a hand
wearily through his hair, he said, 'Your secret's safe with
me.'

He and Paula Kincaid stood there, stiffly, without
speaking again, till Sara and Zach came back.

Sara didn't look at him as she passed to get to the
boat. Nor did she look at him as they zoomed away.

But Logan stood there, watching, till long after the
sleek white cabin cruiser had disappeared over the ho-
rizon.

Zach and Paula were commendably tactful regarding
Sara's relationship with Logan, and when she made it
clear she didn't want to discuss it, or him, they respected

her wish and the whole interlude was placed and kept out of bounds.

But still Sara sensed her mother's natural curiosity, and she was glad when Zach and Paula returned to Los Angeles in late July, and she could once more be on her own.

After she'd left Travis, she'd rented a small apartment in Kitsilano, but she'd taken very little with her from her old life. She had, of course, taken all the Sally Cole sweaters she'd knitted during the early years, but she'd never felt up to unpacking them.

At the beginning of August, she made a start on doing just that. Unpacking and sorting. And she also began searching for a store to rent.

The only place she could afford was run-down and dirty. But the location was good, on a busy side street adjacent to South Granville, near a block of high-class boutiques.

She took possession on September the first, and spent the next three days scrubbing the store from top to bottom, including the kitchen cubbyhole and the small toilet.

On the fourth day, she got up early, put on an old T-shirt and shorts, and with the trunk of her blue Toyota Cressida packed with pots of white paint, brushes, rollers, and all the other paraphernalia she would need to paint the walls, she drove from her apartment building to the store.

Next to it was Hamburger Heaven…a greasy-looking set-up to be sure, but the owner made the best hamburgers for miles around. Perhaps, she decided as she parked the car, she would go in there that evening for dinner.

If she covered as much ground as she intended to today, she'd be much too tired to cook when she got home.

'Excuse me, Mr Hunter…'

Logan frowned as the office receptionist addressed him from around the corner of the boardroom door. His annual September board meeting had a heavy agenda to be covered, and he'd left strict instructions not to be disturbed.

'Yes, Marianne?' he asked brusquely. 'What is it?'

'It's your daughter, Mr Hunter. She'd like to have a word…'

Logan's frown eased. Marianne had standing instructions that, no matter how busy he was, if Andy phoned, he'd be available to take her call.

He got to his feet. 'Take five,' he said to the assembled group, and strode out of the room.

'Line one, Mr Hunter,' Marianne called over her shoulder as she returned to the front desk.

'Right.' Logan went into his office and shut the door. Hitching his hip on the edge of his desk, he picked up the phone.

'Yeah, sweetie, what is it?'

'Guess what, Dad?' Andy's voice was high with excitement. 'I was just reading this tabloid—'

'*Tabloid*? Why aren't you in school?'

He heard her exaggeratedly patient sigh. 'Daddy, it's a PD day—I told you. I'm at home.'

These damned Professional Development days; all they did was give the teachers a day out of the classroom and give the kids time on their hands, time to get into mischief. 'Oh, yeah. OK, so what was so important you had to drag me from my meeting?'

'Zach Grant.' Her voice was taut with suppressed excitement. 'He's been married...for two years...to "that woman's" mother! Can you believe it?'

Logan rolled his eyes. For *this* he was putting his board meeting on hold? Ye gods!

'Andy—' he tried to keep his frustration from showing in his voice '—can we talk about this earth-shaking news tonight? And...the lady's name is Mrs Wynter, not "that woman". I explained to you when you got back from Galiano that I'd been totally wrong about her.' He *had* explained—but he'd been careful not to give away Zach Grant's secret.

'Yeah, she's Sally Cole. Chrissie nearly choked when I told her!' Andy giggled at the memory. 'But I was going to phone you anyway just now, to remind you it's Mrs P's day off and you promised to take me to Hamburger Heaven for dinner. Don't be late. I'll be waiting.'

They hung up, but Logan found himself in no hurry to return to his board meeting. Instead, he found his thoughts drifting back...

After Sara had left the island, he'd thrown himself again into readying the house for sale. Andy had already chosen what she wanted of her mother's personal items; he'd arranged to have them transported to the mainland, along with all the furniture, which was to be auctioned off.

On her return from Galiano, Andy had asked him if she could have her mother's portrait, and Logan had told her she could...eventually; but the prestigious artist who had painted it had been pressing Logan to let him hang the canvas in his Robson Street gallery, on a long-term basis, and Logan had finally agreed.

He'd felt much heartache as he'd seen the portrait go, but he'd been sure he was doing the right thing. He needed to make a break with the past and move on; this was the first step.

But things hadn't gone as he'd planned.

First of all, his place on Madronna hadn't sold.

'Over-priced,' his top agent had said with a sniff. 'You know it, Logan…just as you know damned well that setting your initial price too high is a mistake of the first water.' She'd waggled a thin, puce-tipped finger at him. 'And I know that you've set the price too high because you just don't want the place to sell!'

He'd murmured evasively…but of course she'd been right. Deep down, he *didn't* want the property to sell. One day he'd have to bite the bullet and lower the price; one day, but not yet…

Secondly, his quest for a wife was doomed to failure.

Oh, he did, determinedly, take women out. Women he met through friends, or at work, or by chance.

So far, he'd never made it past the dinner stage.

First there'd been Brenna, who, he'd discovered over dessert, brayed like a deranged donkey at his weakest jokes.

Then there was Pansy, sweet as her name over pre-prandial drinks…but voracious as a barracuda as she'd ripped greedily into her blood-red steak.

Pansy was followed by Raven, all black hair and white skin and scarlet lips…who'd told him, and everyone else within earshot in the five-star dining room, that she was wearing no undies and wanted him to take her, right there and then, on the wall-to-wall patterned Axminster carpet.

Briony had pouty pink lips, blonde hair, earrings bigger than her IQ, and no head for wine. She'd passed out in the Mercedes as he'd driven her home from the restaurant.

Cilla had seemed perfect. Her laughter was soft, her eating style dainty, her panty-line unmistakable, her liquor intake nil. But over dinner he'd discovered the lady was interested in only one topic...upon which she'd enlarged at great length and in a foreign tongue. As she'd gushed, 'Bruno Magli...Escada...and Louis Fèraud,' his eyes had glazed over; when she'd gushed, 'Ferragamo...Versace...and Karl Lagerfeld, Gianfranco Ferré and Chanel,' he'd mentally bade her adieu.

That was two weeks ago, and he hadn't ventured out on a date since.

Till tonight.

Tonight he had a date with his daughter.

What did *that* say about his social life? Pretty damned bleak, he admitted. And bleak was the way he felt most of the time, anyway.

Oh, he managed to put on a front when he was with Andy; but that was all it was—a front.

And tonight he'd have to put on that front again. To please his daughter.

Hamburger Heaven yet!

He straightened his tie, pushed himself off the desk, wished this meeting were over so he could take off his jacket. He could feel the sweat running down his back, soaking his shirt.

It was the hottest September on record, bar none!

*   *   *

Sara felt like a piece of limp lettuce.

She looked down at her paint-splattered clothes: *white* lettuce?

But at least she had given the whole place its undercoat. She looked around the store, with its old-fashioned curved window, and its nooks at either side. She had always seen possibilities in the place, from the first moment she'd stepped inside; and now, with the white walls brightening it, she felt her spirits rise a notch.

Today, she had brought the Sally Cole boutique one step nearer to reality.

She had left the back door open all day, a door that led out to a lane. Adjacent to the door was a small patch of earth that she envisaged, next summer, as a sunny mini-garden—planted with geraniums—where she would eat lunch.

She crossed to the door to get some air...and was treated to another whiff of the oniony smell that had been tantalising her for the past hour. From Hamburger Heaven.

But could she go in there, looking the way she did?

She smiled tiredly. Why not? She was too darned hungry to care who saw her. Besides, nobody *she* knew would stoop to eating dinner in such a greasy spoon!

Logan parked his silver Mercedes convertible in the rear lane behind Hamburger Heaven, next to a blue Toyota.

Andy bubbled away happily as they walked along the lane, and round to the street entrance. 'I'm going to pig out, Dad. I'm just starving; I'm going to order a...'

Hardly listening to her, Logan pushed open the door. Andy squeezed in front of him through the crowd in the small entryway, and they made for the counter, where a frazzled hostess was taking names.

When she reached Andy, Andy said, 'Hunter, table for two.'

'You're looking at a three-quarter-hour wait.' The hostess snapped her gum. 'We're *real* busy tonight.'

Andy looked disappointedly up at her father.

'What do you think, Dad? Should we go and get a takeout? Dad? *Dad?*' She waved her hand in front of his face. 'What are you looking at?'

'What I am looking at,' he said, his eyes fixed on the paint-splattered creature taking up sole occupancy of a booth-for-four and tucking ravenously into the largest hamburger he'd ever seen, 'is Mrs Sara Wynter—'

'Miss!' The hostess sounded irritable. 'You want me to put you down, or not?'

'Not,' Logan said to her. 'Thanks.'

With Andy right behind him, he weaved his way to the quarter-occupied booth. He stopped by it, and put an arm round Andy's shoulders.

He cleared his throat. 'Excuse me,' he said mildly, 'would you mind if my daughter and I joined you?'

CHAPTER EIGHT

SARA'S heart gonged against her ribs with such a bang, it knocked the breath from her lungs.

Logan Hunter.

Ye gods, she'd just been thinking about the man!

Well, *that* wasn't so unusual; after all, hardly a moment passed that she didn't think of him, despite her efforts to blank him from her mind. And now here he was—looking sinfully attractive in an emerald-green T-shirt and black shorts—while *she*—well, she could just imagine what she looked like, flushed scarlet and spotted with white paint! Why, oh, why had she not driven home instead of—?

'Sara?' Logan sounded amused. 'Have pity, for Pete's sake! There's not a free table, and Andy's starving—'

'And for once Dad let me have my way and promised we'd eat here,' Andy interjected. 'It's, like, a *real* treat for me and he hardly ever gives in. He's, like, big on health food at the moment.' She fixed her eyes pleadingly on Sara.

Cornered. 'Sure.' Sara choked out the word as she slid over the bench. Her heartbeats jammed when Logan made to sit beside her, and she quickly patted the seat and said, 'Sit here, Andy. Let's give your dad the other bench to himself so he'll have more room.'

'Thanks.' Andy sat down and as she did she ran a curious glance over Sara's outfit.

'I've…er…been painting,' Sara explained, watching

Logan take the opposite bench. A crafty move, she decided, to seat him there; the last thing she wanted was him right next to her, with his granite thighs pressing close to hers.

He slid over till he was by the window. Directly opposite her. And his knees touched hers.

Sara gulped, but controlled the automatic urge to part her legs and escape his touch; somehow that would have made her feel even more vulnerable to the man than she already did. Definitely not an option.

He grinned across at her.

'What's so funny?' she asked defensively.

He leaned across the table and rubbed the tip of her nose. 'Paint,' he said. 'It's in your hair too.'

'Dad—' Andy took the menu the waiter handed her '—it's very rude to make personal remarks.' She glanced at the waiter. 'I'll have the double Heaven, fries, coleslaw, potato salad, and a large Coke. Thanks.' She handed back the menu, and said to Sara, 'He seems to forget his manners when he's around you. Does he ever apologise?'

Logan waved away the menu proffered by the waiter. 'Double Heaven and a coffee, thanks.'

'Yes,' Sara said, 'he does sometimes apologise—'

'But she doesn't always accept my apologies.' Logan's tone was light, but as their eyes met Sara knew he was remembering their last confrontation, on the jetty.

'Perhaps she has a bit of a temper,' Sara said, matching his light tone, 'and perhaps later she realises she was too quick off the mark.'

'Perhaps she would like to get together some time and talk about it?' Logan's eyes had darkened.

Sara hesitated, and while she did the waiter brought

Logan's coffee and Andy's Coke. After he left, Andy started chattering about Zach, and the moment passed. Sara didn't know whether to feel relieved or disappointed that she hadn't had to answer Logan's question.

The teenager wanted to know all about Zach and Sara's mother, and now that the secret of their relationship was out Sara was free to talk about it.

'My mother went to work for Zach about five years ago,' she said. 'And it wasn't long before they fell in love. But Zach had to keep to the terms of his contract...'

'I know,' Andy said. 'He had to go out with all these models and make it seem like he was such a swinger. But now he's finished that contract it's OK. How does it feel, Sara, to have him for a stepdad?'

'I don't really think of him like that, Andy. He's a friend. A good friend. My father died when I was fifteen, and nobody will ever take his place. But Zach doesn't want to, so it's all worked out just fine.'

'I don't want a stepmom.' Andy sat back as the waiter served her food and Logan's. 'But I don't have to worry about it. My dad'll never marry again. We're a team, the two of us. We don't need anybody else.'

Sara didn't know why she felt as if Andy had thrown a bucket of cold water over her, but she did. She darted a glance at Logan. He was staring out of the window, his lips compressed, his expression distant. It was as if Andy's casually tossed-out words had spoiled his mood too.

Sara had been picking at her burger since the two had joined her; now she no longer felt remotely hungry.

She pushed her plate to the side and murmured, 'If

you'll excuse me, I have to leave.' She signalled to their waiter.

Logan frowned. 'What's the rush? Hang on a bit. You haven't even told us what you're doing—'

The waiter came over. 'Will this all be on one cheque?'

'Yes,' Logan said quickly.

Sara watched as the waiter filled in the bill. But when he held it across to Logan she flicked it away.

'This is on me,' she said, tucking a tip under her plate. And could have hugged Andy who slid off the bench and allowed her to get out without any fuss.

'Thanks, Andy,' she said, and managed a smile.

Logan had stood up. 'Sara—'

'Goodbye, Logan. It was nice seeing you both again.'

She wove her way through the crowds to the front desk where she was fortunate enough to be attended to right away. She handed over the bill and the correct change, and was out of Hamburger Heaven quicker than a flash.

She stole a glance back as the glass door swung shut behind her…and her heart lurched when she saw that Logan was trying to work his way through the crowd after her.

She was panting by the time she got to her car. She threw herself into it and took off down the lane like a bat from hell. When she turned onto South Granville, an anxious peek into her rear-view mirror confirmed that she wasn't being followed.

It also confirmed that she was looking an absolute mess. And she couldn't even begin to imagine why a man like Logan Hunter would be interested in chasing after her!

*   *   *

'Dad, aren't you going to finish your burger?'

'What?' Logan gathered his scattered thoughts, and looked across the table at his daughter. 'Oh…yeah, sure.'

'Mrs Wynter…Sara…wasn't it funny meeting her here? I wonder what she was painting?' Andy chuckled. 'I bet she hated for you to see her like that. Women do. Can you imagine Mom ever going out like that? Actually, I can't imagine Mom would ever have come to a place like this.'

Logan hid his surprise. He couldn't recall Andy ever bringing up the subject of her mother. Surely this was a good sign, and something he should encourage?

'Your mom?' Logan glanced around. 'Well, yeah, she'd have come if you'd wanted her to. You had her twisted round your little finger, sweetie.'

'Mmm.' Andy's expression was reflective. 'But I don't think she would've actually *chosen* to come here. Dad, want to take a drive past the old place after we eat?'

Though the words had been spoken in an offhand manner, Logan sensed a tension in them. But he didn't let Andy realise he'd noticed, nor did he show his further surprise at her request. He himself had never gone near their old home since the day they'd left it five years ago; and he doubted very much that Andy had either.

'Oh, sure.' He kept his voice vague, as if he were barely paying attention. 'Sure, we can do that. It might be interesting to see what they've done with the gardens. Your mother's rose garden in particular.'

'That was her favourite place, wasn't it, Dad—Mom's rose garden? I used to love sitting on the swing there, watching her pruning, or weeding—or talking to the roses!'

But Logan was only half listening as his own thoughts drifted back.

Within weeks of Bethany's death, unable to cope with the memories they had so lovingly built into their Point Grey home, he'd sold the property.

He'd rented a condo—in the same general area, so Andy wouldn't have to change schools. He'd meant it as a temporary measure, but somehow he'd never got around to buying again. He'd kept putting it off, though once in a while he'd looked at a place that caught his fancy...

Just as, once in a while, he'd looked at a woman.

But though he'd dated once or twice, always with his promise to Bethany in his mind, he'd never met anyone he could seriously envisage spending the rest of his life with.

'Just imagine,' Andy was murmuring, 'Sara having Zach Grant as a stepdad!'

Sara.

He could imagine spending the rest of his life with Sara Wynter.

And wasn't that a laugh, considering he'd pegged her from the beginning as the woman he'd *least* want to marry?

But, seeing her this evening, he'd been stunned by the rush of pleasure she'd excited in him.

How long was it since he'd felt that kind of lifting of his spirits?

Not since that day they'd spent sailing.

The day she'd told him her views on marriage. She'd been adamant she'd never marry again...but that was because her first marriage had been a mistake. The union had been based on romantic notions, rather than on practicalities.

He didn't want to marry either, but for different reasons. He was a one-woman man, and Bethany had been that woman. But then…there was his promise.

And then…there was Andy, badly needing a mother.

Oh, the child would deny that, vehemently. But she did need a maternal figure in her life…and she seemed to like Sara. And surely the fact that she'd have Zach Grant as her—what? Step-step-grandfather?—would sweeten the pill.

Only problem was…he didn't know where she lived. He had to admit that out of curiosity he'd looked up her name in the Vancouver phone book, after he and Andy had returned from Madronna at the end of July. It hadn't been listed.

'Dad.' Andy sucked up the last of her Coke with her straw. 'Thanks, that was really good.'

'Ready to go?'

'Yeah, I'm ready.'

They left Hamburger Heaven and strolled in the warm evening around to the back lane.

He was backing the Mercedes out of the parking spot, when he chanced to glance at the rear of the store next door to Hamburger Heaven.

Through the sparkling clean window, he had a clear view of three objects sitting on the wide sill inside: a paint pot with dried white paint striating the label; a roller with its fuzzy pad washed clean; and a roller pan propped against the frame, its metal surface winking at the sun.

In his mind's eye, he saw the delectable Mrs Wynter,

her nose, her hair and her clothes all spattered with white paint.

Even a fool would have been able to figure out the connection.

And Logan Hunter was no fool!

Next afternoon, Sara knocked off at five, after having spent the day giving the walls another two coats of paint.

She'd just come out of the tiny bathroom after washing the roller and tray, when she saw a silver convertible pulling in beside her Toyota.

Possibly the Hamburger Heaven car park was full. She didn't mind their customers using her few spaces…at the moment. But once she opened her store that would be a different matter.

She set the roller and tray on the windowsill, leaning them against the frame, then she turned her back to the window and looked around at the walls. They were drying already, and the place looked lovely and fresh.

She'd left the rear door open all day again to let the paint fumes out, and through it she now heard a car door open, and slam shut. Then footsteps on the cement surface. She lifted clumps of her long hair from her nape, let the breeze drift coolingly over her heated skin.

The footsteps weren't fading, as they should have done. She frowned as they became louder. The tread was heavy. A man's. He was wearing shoes, rather than sneakers. And now the sound was very close—

She spun round, her hands still at her nape.

A man stood in the doorway.

He was tall, with wide shoulders, long legs. Blinded by the brightness from the lane, she could see nothing else. But a second before the intruder spoke she knew who he was.

'Tonight,' Logan said, 'dinner is on me.'

'Logan.' Sara felt dazed. Shaking her head, she said, 'I'm sorry. I couldn't stomach another Heavenly hamburger so soon. But thanks anyway.'

She dropped her hands, and folded her arms around herself. And wished she were wearing something more substantial than her skimpy old tube top and shorts.

'I had something more...civilised...in mind.' He came forward, and looked around. 'You've done a good job. When's the grand opening?'

Above the smell of paint, the scent of his aftershave came to her. She wanted to close her eyes, savour it; it was absolutely *delicious*...

She wondered if her sweaty scent was drifting to him! He'd probably find it sexy; she'd read that men did. Her stomach did a butterfly flip at the notion. Was he, at this very moment, getting turned on?

'First of October. If all goes well.'

'You'll invite me, of course.'

'I hadn't thought of—'

'You will. But for now shall we go? I assume that's your blue car out back. I'll follow you to your place, give you a few minutes to shower and change... Have you any thinners?'

She gaped. 'Well, yes...through there—' she nodded '—in the bathroom.'

He strode past her, came back bearing the tin of turps, and a paper towel.

'Come here.' He beckoned her over to the window.

'I thought I'd gotten most of it off,' she said weakly.

'Over here.'

She went.

And stood, like a child, with her face up to him as he gently cleaned spots of white paint from her brow, and from her nose.

'There.' He smiled down at her, and his breath was minty-fresh. 'Perfect again.'

Her heart stammered. 'Thanks.'

'My pleasure.'

She could have stood there for ever, counting his every black eyelash, every fine line crinkling out from his eyes as he smiled. She could also have put her arms around his waist and set her cheek against his heart…but she didn't.

She stepped back.

He returned to the bathroom with the turps and paper towel, and she leaned against the counter, reeling mentally. By the time he came back, she should have managed to gather herself together, but she still felt intoxicated, as if she'd been tippling champagne. Just looking at him made her giddy; he was wearing a dress shirt with a thin navy and white stripe, a red tie, and crisp grey flannels…and when he threw her a smile her throat became as dry as the Sahara. 'Right.' He scooped up her handbag from the paint sheet in the corner. 'Just give me your address, in case we should get separated, and let's be on our way.'

They did become separated. And he must have taken a short cut, because when she turned into her street she saw his Mercedes parked outside her apartment building. He was standing leaning against the luxurious vehicle.

She parked behind him, and got out.

'Would you like to come up,' she asked, 'or would you prefer to wait out here?'

To her surprise, he said, 'I've been stuck indoors all day. I'll take a walk in the park over there.' He shot up his cuff, and glanced at his watch. 'Twenty minutes?'

She nodded, and turned away.

'And,' he called after her, 'wear something glitzy. This is going to be one very special dinner.'

Glitzy.

She'd give him glitzy!

Sara opened her closet door and took out the dress Paula had brought her when she and Zach had come up to Vancouver in late June. Paula had bought it on Rodeo Drive, but had refused to divulge what it had cost. The label said Valentino. Sara had stared in awe.

Now she draped the dress out on the bed. It was cobalt silk, a slip of a thing on the hanger, but on the body— sheer dynamite!

She wished—

Oh, she wished, wistfully, that if Logan had wanted to take her out he'd have wanted to do something…simpler. Memories of Travis were crushing in on her.

'For God's sake, Sara, you wore that dress last month at the charity do in the Pan Pacific! Didn't I tell you to get something new for this theatre show? It's not as if we can't afford it, dammit! And the bottom line is we have to impress people. It's not enough to be successful…we have to be seen to be successful!'

Sara shivered. Travis…and Logan.

On the island, Logan had seemed so different from her ex-husband. Logan had enjoyed the things she had that day on the beach, when they'd swum, and played Frisbee, and picnicked, and talked...

But she'd hardly got a chance to know him! And now they were back in the city...and he was, after all, a city man.

A successful man.

A businessman.

And, like Travis, he had an image to present.

Well, she wanted no part of it. Oh, tonight she'd go along with it—she'd have to; she was in it right up to her neck—but only because he'd caught her off guard. He'd disarmed her with his charm...and conquered her with his tenderness, when he'd cleaned the paint off her face.

Tonight, he was probably paying a debt. He felt he owed her, because she'd paid the bill at Hamburger Heaven, and, being a male chauvinist, he wouldn't find that easy to swallow.

But after tonight they'd be all square again.

And she would make sure it stayed that way.

'Wow!' Logan's voice greeted her as she walked outside.

He came forward and his green eyes were warm. They caressed her and her skin tingled wherever they touched. 'You're something else, Mrs Sara Wynter.'

He must have had a blazer in the car; he was wearing it now, and as she looked at him she felt something akin to pain. A longing, a wanting. Exquisite to the point of being unbearable.

'You're something else yourself, Mr Hunter,' she said, the faintest tremble in her voice.

He took her hand and led her to the car. His fingers

clasped hers firmly, confidently. And she wanted them to stay there, for ever. She wanted him to say, Why don't we forget dinner? Let's just go for a walk in the park, and find a cosy bench, and sit and talk...

Of course, he didn't.

The interior of the Mercedes was de luxe, with plush upholstery, a wonderful 'new' smell, and a dashboard that made her think of an airplane cockpit. Everything was complex, and shiny, and of top quality.

'Do you mind,' he asked, 'if I catch the news?'

'Not at all.' So...he didn't want to talk. That figured. This was Logan Hunter, successful businessman out on a date.

Sara sank back in her seat and looked out of the window. She wanted to ask where they were going, but he was concentrating on listening to the radio.

She leaned back and closed her eyes. Lord, she was tired. All that painting had exhausted her. She put her fingers over her mouth to cover a yawn.

'Here we are.'

She came to with a jerk.

'Heavens—' she sat up straight '—I must have nodded off. How long have I been—?'

'Just a few minutes.' He unsnapped his belt buckle, and, reaching over, unsnapped hers.

She saw they were in a residential area. And parked outside a condo building she recognised as one of the most pricey in the Lower Mainland.

She snapped her head round and stared at him.

'I assumed we were going to a restaurant,' she said.

'Uh-uh.'

'You're taking me to a private party?'

He got out, rounded the car, opened her door.

'Come on,' he said. 'We don't want to be late.'

'Where are you taking me?' she asked weakly.

He grinned.

'You'll find out—' he slammed her door and put his hand in the small of her back '—when we get there.'

CHAPTER NINE

'So, LIKE I explained,' Andy said as she served Sara coffee from an elegant silver pot, 'for my badge I had to prepare a formal dinner for two adults, and then have them sign this form telling my Home Ec teacher it was OK. And when I told Dad he suggested—'

'I suggested that Mrs Sara Wynter might be pleased to be a guinea pig.'

'Dad!'

'Don't tease, Logan!' Sara smiled up at Andy, who was hovering nervously behind her. 'You did a super job...and that cheesecake...mmm, it was yummy! I'd love to have the recipe!' She glanced at Logan. 'I'm glad I could come, but what would you have done if I'd had another engagement?'

Andy said, 'Oh, Mrs Pappagopolous was standing by.' She rounded the table and served her father's coffee. 'She's our housekeeper. Dad told her, before he went to fetch you, that if she didn't hear from him within the half-hour she was to take the evening off. And she didn't, so she did.'

Logan looked up at his daughter. 'You did a great job, Andy. That was one terrific meal.'

'Thanks, Dad.' She bent and gave him a peck on the cheek. 'Now, if you'll excuse me, I'm going to get started on the dishes.'

'Oh, let me help with those,' Sara offered quickly.

'I wish you could,' Andy said over her shoulder as

she made for the door, 'but I have to do everything myself. Like, *everything*! Thanks anyway.'

She went out, letting the door swing shut behind her. Sara looked across the table at Logan.

'Andy is a very lucky girl,' she said.

'How so?'

'You're doing a wonderful job of bringing her up.'

'I can't take all the credit,' he said. 'She's her mother's daughter, and the eight years they had together…that's where her sweetness comes from…'

'Oh, you're pretty sweet yourself, Logan Hunter.'

He grinned, and Sara thought he suddenly looked ten years younger. 'Sweet and charming! Now *there*'s a fatal combination…and I intend on making the most of it!' He rose, still smiling. 'How about we take our coffee outside? May as well enjoy this Indian summer before the rains come.'

The verandah was high above the city, and faced west. The air was warm, and scented by the tubs of plants set around the cedar floor. Sara sat on a cushioned swing, and as she started it gently rocking Logan put his cup down on a side table, shucked off his blazer, and sat down beside her.

'It's a pity,' he said softly, 'that the kitchen looks out on the balcony.'

Frowning, Sara turned to look at him. 'Why so?'

'Because—' his gaze dropped to her lips '—I want to kiss you.'

She heard the swift intake of her breath.

'Desperately,' he added.

Her cup rattled in its saucer. He relieved her of both, placed them on the table. 'We wouldn't want you to spill,' he murmured, 'on that very slinky dress.' He took her nearer hand in his, and set it on his thigh. 'So tell me, Mrs Sara Wynter, how do you feel about…kissing?'

'You mean—' she sounded as if someone was pressing a fingertip against her windpipe '—in…general terms?'

'No. Specific terms. As in…us kissing.'

'What do you mean…what do I think about it?'

'Well, are you for it…or agin it?'

'You mean…now?'

'No, I mean…later.'

She tried to say something, but it came out in a mumble.

'Was that a no?' he asked lightly.

She shook her head. 'No, it was an "Oh".'

'As in "Oh, yes"? Or as in "Oh, no"? Or as in "Oh, maybe"?'

'As in "Oh, I really don't want to be having this conversation!"'

He chuckled. 'Well, that's what I get for asking—'

The screen door behind them opened.

Sara quickly slipped her hand from Logan's grasp, and he made no attempt to detain her. Andy was very possessive about her father, and Sara sensed his unspoken agreement that it wouldn't do to mar the evening by having Andy see them holding hands.

'There,' Andy said. 'The dishes are in the dishwasher. I can sit with you for a while.'

Sara reached for her cup and saucer, and sipped some coffee as the teenager plonked herself down on a chair.

'So—' Andy looked from Logan to Sara '—what are we going to do for the rest of the evening?'

'What would *you* like to do, Andy?' Sara asked.

'Oh, I've got tons of homework lined up. I meant, what are *you* guys going to do?'

'Actually—' Sara glanced at her watch '—I wouldn't mind getting home soon. I'd like to have an early night…'

'Andy, why don't you bring out those forms and we'll sign them? Then Sara and I can be on our way.'

'And don't forget the dessert recipe,' Sara added. 'I'd like to scribble a copy before we go.'

She knew by the sudden flush on Andy's cheeks that the teenager was gratified to be asked again for the recipe. What Sara hadn't expected was the impulsive gesture Andy made at the moment of their leaving.

They were all three standing by the bank of elevators, and the doors of the nearest one had just glided open, when Andy said, 'Bye, then…and Sara, thanks for coming. It was a fun evening.' Then came the hug.

Startled, Sara was about to hug her back, but Andy had already slipped away and was running lightly back along the carpeted corridor.

Logan walked Sara to the door of her apartment building.

He sensed she was in a hurry to get away from him. And when she took the key from her purse her fingers trembled.

He found it endearing that she should be shy with him.

He found everything about her endearing.

In her elegant blue dress, with her blonde hair swirled up, she looked like a model—but models were cool and distant. There had been no mistaking Sara's genuine delight when she'd discovered they were to be eating dinner in his home, a dinner prepared and served by his daughter. And the way she'd been with Andy had touched him.

He heard the sound of the key turning in the lock. He put his hand over hers, stopping her.

She looked up, her expression startled.

'You know,' he murmured, 'there's only one thing wrong with having dinner served by a minor.'

'What's that?'

'No booze.'

Sara chuckled. 'Yes, I suppose the cranberry cocktail before the meal wasn't what you would have chosen...'

'I could be persuaded,' he said lazily, 'to come up for a nightcap.'

He saw alarm in her eyes.

'Well...' she said.

He uttered a mock-groan. 'Oh, for Pete's sake don't let's start that again. Give me either a yes or a no!'

She screwed up her nose. 'Yes?'

'That's the most indecisive yes I've ever heard!' He removed the key from the lock and shoved it into her bag. 'Let's get inside before you change your mind!'

Her apartment was on the fourth floor, and the view, he discovered when he crossed to the sitting-room window, consisted of the flat roof of a supermarket, a parking area with a dumpster, and a narrow dusty lane.

'It's dismal, isn't it?' Sara remarked. 'But I'm first on the waiting list for an apartment on the other side of the building, overlooking the park. That'll be nicer. So—' she tossed down her bag '—what would you like to drink?'

The sitting room was bright, with comfortable-looking furniture, tall bookcases taking up most of one wall, and a stand with TV and stereo in the corner adjacent to the window. He found it a pleasingly uncluttered room, yet it had a homely charm. He wanted to scan the bookshelves, find out what she liked to read...but that would wait.

He smiled. 'Let's see what you've got.'

He followed her through to a galley-style kitchenette. And when she reached up to open a cupboard he forgot all about her books and became mesmerised by the lovely curve of her nape, and the silky upswept coil of her blonde hair.

Peeking from the coil was a sterling-silver clasp.

Which he would, he decided, undo at the first possible opportunity, and let that rich hair tumble down her back.

'Ah—' he reached past her '—Drambuie. Same for you?'

'No, I'll have the Tia Maria.' She provided two heavy crystal liqueur glasses.

He carried their drinks back to the sitting room.

'This is a one-bedroom place?' He sank down onto a low-slung love seat opposite the armchair she'd chosen.

'Yes.' She kicked off her pumps, tucked her feet under her.

'You moved in here after your divorce?'

'Oh, long before the divorce. I moved in here right after I found out Travis was having an affair.'

He could see she meant to sound casual, but her fingers had tightened around the stem of her glass.

'The old story,' he said. 'But that doesn't make it any easier to bear...'

'And what made it worse—' She stopped short, and shook her head. He thought he saw a glimmer of tears.

He put down his glass. 'Worse? What the hell could

be worse than finding out that your husband had be-
trayed you?'

'There's more than one kind of betrayal— I'm
sorry—' she dropped her gaze '—I don't want to talk
about it.'

'You're sure? Sometimes it helps…'

She shook her head again. 'No. Nothing could help.'

Silence stretched between them. She took another sip
of her drink, and another. Quickly, as if desperately
keeping herself occupied, so she wouldn't have to talk.
She finished the liqueur…while he hadn't even started
his. Realising she needed a few moments to gather herself together, he got up, his hands clenched into fists,
and walked over to the bookcases.

What else could that rat have done to have upset her
so much? Could he have physically abused her? The
thought made his blood boil.

He forced himself to concentrate on the hundreds of
books arranged—alphabetically!—on the many shelves.

'I see you're a Ludlum fan.' The nail of his index
finger made a rippling sound as he ran it slowly across
the spines of glossy hardbacks and fat paperbacks.
'Kellerman, King, Ludlum, MacInnes, Pilcher, Puzo,
Rendell—'

He turned, and was relieved to see that on the surface,
at any rate, she'd regained her composure. 'Are you this
organised in every aspect of your life?' he teased.

She rose from her chair. He saw the silk dress lick
her breasts and hips as she walked towards him. He felt
the tiger roar. He didn't try to discipline it.

She stopped beside him, her attention on the novels.
'Some people collect teaspoons,' she said, 'others collect
corkscrews, some collect art. Books are my weak-

ness—and my joy. And I like to have them tidy.' She glanced up at him, a faint mockery in her eyes. 'I'm not a neat freak, though. Unlike you!'

'Me?'

'Your kitchen drawers…in your house on the island…a place for everything, and everything in its place.'

'Not guilty, m'lud! That was the first time I'd been on the island for five years. Bethany was the neat freak. I'm just your run-of-the-mill slob!'

As always, when he talked of Bethany, his voice had softened. Sara must have noticed, because she said, 'Isn't it odd that neither of us will marry again…but for such different reasons? You because your first marriage was so happy, and I because mine was—' She shrugged.

'What makes you think I don't plan to marry again?'

Her brow wrinkled, and he knew he'd confused her.

'Well,' she said hesitantly, 'because of what Andy said.'

He leaned back against the bookcase, and, taking her by the shoulders, pulled her close. Because of his laid-back angle, she ended up lying against him, with the full pressure of her lower body against his. It was arousing. To the point of discomfort. He cleared his throat.

'Andy doesn't want things to change,' he said. 'She has convinced herself that we're a twosome, and that neither of us will ever need anyone else.'

'But she didn't seem to object to your bringing me for dinner.'

'That's because—' Logan kissed the tiny chickenpox indentation on her brow '—she's confident I won't re-marry so she doesn't see you…or any other woman…as a threat.'

Was she a threat? he asked himself. Certainly to his peace of mind! Right now, he wanted to sweep her up in his arms and stride with her to wherever her bedroom was. He managed to contain himself...but for how much longer he wasn't sure. The tiger was roaring to be let loose. 'Know something?' he said huskily. 'I made a mistake, earlier.'

'What?'

'When I asked you if you were for or agin kissing.'

'That was a mistake?'

'Yeah. I shouldn't have asked.'

He was a man who never made the same mistake twice. This time, he didn't ask. He took.

Her lips were soft and tasted of coffee. She stiffened, as if about to resist, but when he moved his lips over hers, passionately, she moaned and slid her arms around his neck. She clung there, as if her ankles had given way. And her lips clung to his, her response honest and giving.

As his kiss deepened, he felt her fingertips dig into his nape. Felt her breasts tighten. Swell. And he felt a tightening in his groin.

He savoured the pleasure, the pleasure that was so intense it was akin to pain, and set himself to prolonging it.

The tiger's roar quietened to somewhere between an appreciative growl and a contented purr.

'I'll have you know,' he whispered after a very long time, 'that *The Parsifal Mosaic* is jutting into my spine.'

Her breath caught in a half-laugh. 'We should move...'

'Somewhere comfortable...' He pushed himself from

the bookcase, at the same time sweeping her up in his arms as if she were a wisp of gossamer.

She buried her face against his neck, and he felt the heat of her skin.

Heartbeats drumming, he strode out into the hallway. Through an open doorway, he saw her bedroom…and made for it like a lemming to the sea.

The room was bright—the carpet gold, the walls crisp Wedgwood-blue, the ceiling painted yellow. Sunshine filtered through the window's filmy white sheers, giving everything a golden glow. The window itself was open a few inches and from outside drifted the sound of a stereo. Country music—a slow, sad song of lost love and betrayal.

He stopped by the bed and slid her to her feet, letting her feel each hard ridge of his body on the way down.

He heard her ragged gasp of awareness. It excited him further. He kissed her again, and she met hungry kiss with hungry kiss. Without raising his lips for an instant, he took the clasp from her hair; the rich strands fell like silk around his wrists. He disentangled himself, and slid the clasp into his hip pocket.

He reached around to undo the long back zip of her dress; the dress slithered to the carpet.

She stepped out of it.

And they tumbled together onto the bed.

All around him was her scent…in her hair, on her skin, in the sheets. It intoxicated him, and blotted out the rest of the world.

'I want to ask you something.' His voice had thickened. 'Are you for, or agin?'

'What?'

'This…'

Her pupils were so dark, so dilated, the irises had all but disappeared. 'You should have asked me earlier...'

'I'm asking you now...'

Cheeks flushed, eyes glazed, she worked open the knot of his tie, unthreaded the tie from his shirt collar, and dropped it on the carpet.

'Too late,' she whispered. 'It's out of my hands.'

And it was.

She had fallen in love with him.

It had crept up on her, sneaked up on her, without her once suspecting what was happening. She certainly hadn't been looking for it, wasn't even sure when she first knew it for fact, or even if she welcomed it...

But as Logan engaged her mouth in another steamy kiss she didn't even try to think; instead she gave herself up to sensation. To her throbbing need, and to the wild excitement rushing through her like a summer storm.

She made a throaty sound as he dispensed with her undies; he groaned as she worked off his clothes. Then, naked, they lay face to face, his hands thrust feverishly in her hair as he kissed her again.

She revelled in the male scent of him, in the taste of his salt, in the rasp of his jaw. She revelled in the smooth skin of his back as she ran heated fingers up and down it, and in the hair-roughened skin of his chest as she spread her palms over it. But most of all she revelled in his lips, those searching lips that sipped their way from her mouth to the sensitive area below her ear, over the graceful curve of her shoulder, to the aching peaks so eagerly thrusting for his attention.

Her breath caught as he kissed, and sucked, the beaded tips, spinning exquisite threads to the very core of her, so that she mewed out faint and pleading whimpers.

Whimpers that became husky as, after a long while, he trespassed down over her ribs, and breathless as he trespassed further to the silky triangle adorning her most feminine secret. Arching her head back against the pillows, she wove her fingers tightly into his hair, and gave herself up to pleasure. Intimate pleasure. Unbearable pleasure.

At last, impossibly, she reached the zenith. And she hovered there, quivering, gasping, every nerve aflame, every cell ablaze, before finally, with a cry, she toppled over headlong into a slow-motion fall through space...

She heard him say her name. It echoed in her ears as she pulled him up, pleaded with him to take her, take her now, please take her now...

He made her wait, but only for a moment; she heard the crackle of foil, and knew that this time he was prepared.

Then, with a strangled sound, he claimed her lips again and plunged inside her...drove inside her, each stroke a confirmation of the joy they shared. And when he attained his shuddering climax she was with him every step of the way, and still was with him when they drifted down, down and down again, to a reality that was changed forevermore.

Sara awoke next morning to the sound of someone moving around in her bedroom.

For a second terror slashed through her. She jerked herself upright in the bed, a scream rising in her throat.

A scream that died when she saw Logan at the door.

Her breath rushed out audibly.

Of course. It all came back to her.

Last night came back to her, and shimmering memories, pleasure-tipped memories, arrowed to her heart.

He was dressed, and obviously about to leave; at the sound of her sharp breath, he turned, and in the watery dawn light seeping through the window she saw he was smiling.

'Ah.' He came back into the room, jaw up, fingers working on his tie. 'You're awake.'

Sara inhaled shakily, and pulled the sheet up over her breasts. 'You startled me; I thought—'

'You thought I was a burglar.' He sat on the edge of the mattress and pulled her into his arms. 'I did steal something last night,' he murmured into her hair, and kissed the tousled strands. 'And I'm taking it with me.'

He pulled back and looked into her face.

He had stolen her heart; but he couldn't know that. She ran a fingertip tenderly over his darkly bristled jaw. 'You stole nothing I didn't want to give,' she whispered.

'I stole a sweet memory.' He planted a kiss on the tip of her nose. 'Sweeter than the sweetest wine...and one of many such memories we're going to make together.'

His words stirred Sara from her dreamy reverie. She'd been too besotted with him to think beyond the moment; now she realised she had much thinking to do. About the future. About whether or not it would be wise to see more of this man.

He glanced at his watch and sighed. 'I have to go—I need to be home before Andy gets up.'

Sara nodded.

'But you and I must talk later,' he said. 'I'll call you tonight. You'll be home?'

'Yes, I'll be here.'

'I'm going to have a heart-to-heart with Andy—'

'Do you *have* to? I'd hate for her to be distressed, if it can be avoided.'

He frowned. 'This is not only about last night, Sara. You and I are going to be…seeing each other again.'

He was impatient to leave; she gave him an answer that avoided directly dealing with his implied question. 'Surely, if we were discreet…'

He stood and looked down at her. His eyes were grave.

'I'm not going to sneak around, Sara. It's not my style, and I'm damned well sure it's not yours either. No, she's got to be told what's going on.'

What *is* going on, Logan? Sara wanted to ask as she watched him walk to the door.

Last night, there had been no talk of love. She hadn't expected there to be. Oh, she had given her heart to him, but she knew that Logan Hunter's heart belonged to a ghost—the ghost of his late wife—and always would.

So where did that leave Sara? Did she want to become involved in an open-ended affair, which was surely the most she could ever expect, from this one-woman man?

He turned as he reached the door.

'Just one more thing,' he said, 'and I'd like to have the answer next time I see you.' The serious expression had gone from his eyes; she thought she detected a twinkle.

'What's the question?' She looped her arms around her knees.

'In light of what's happened between us…I want to know if you're for it…or agin it.'

'For…or agin…what?'

'Marriage.'

She stared, hardly believing what she was hearing. 'As in...?'

'You and me, Sara.'

He opened the door and went out, and the door clicked shut behind him. But even as Sara lay back on her pillow, gasping in mouthfuls of air like a dying fish, he opened the door again and poked his head around the edge.

'Myself—' his smile was wolfish '—I'm for it...one hundred per cent!'

CHAPTER TEN

'*DAD!*' Andy's voice came accusingly from the staircase. 'Why are you so *late*?'

Logan froze. Good lord, he hadn't made a sound as he'd entered the condo...which meant that Andy must have waited up for him. He suppressed a groan, substituted a grin.

'Late?' His tone was teasing. 'You mean early, don't you?'

'It's not funny.' Looking younger than her thirteen years in a pink T-shirt nightie, Andy sank down on the fourth from the bottom step, and hugged her arms around her knees as she glared up at him. 'I've been *worried* about you.'

'I'm sorry, honey. I had no idea——Mrs P. came back, didn't she? You weren't alone?'

'Oh, she came back at ten. It wasn't that.'

Logan walked across and, setting one foot on the bottom step, stood looking down at her, his hands in his trouser pockets. 'So...what's the problem?'

She shrugged. 'You were just driving Sara home. What took you so long?'

Oh, lord. Logan extended a hand. 'Let's talk...in the kitchen. I need a cup of coffee.'

She took his hand and he pulled her to her feet.

In the kitchen, she sat cross-legged on one of the cushioned chairs as he set the coffee-maker going.

'Now—' he leaned back against the counter '—let's talk.'

'OK.'

'What do you want to know?'

Her cheeks had taken on a faint peachy tinge. 'Where have you been?'

'With Sara.'

'At her place?'

Logan nodded.

He saw her gaze slice to the clock on the wall behind him. And he knew damned well what time it was. 'I…fell asleep there.' Dammit, he hadn't meant to sound defensive.

'Why didn't Sara just waken you and send you home?'

Was his daughter being deliberately naive…or what?

'Andy, Sara and I have become more than just… friends.'

Still as a statue, she stared at him. He could almost hear her mind working…and he knew the exact moment when the penny dropped: the peachy tinge on her cheeks became scarlet. But even as he watched, and waited, the colour faded to nothing, and her skin took on a waxy look.

'You had *sex* with her?'

Logan winced. The coffee finished dripping, and he turned his back on her, grasping at the excuse to postpone answering.

'Dad?' He heard her slip off her chair, and when he turned she was right behind him, her hands fisted on her hips. His heart sank when he saw that though her chin was tilted defiantly tears glimmered in her eyes.

'Yeah, sweetie?'

'Are you going to *marry* her?' Her voice shook.

His chest rose as he inhaled a deep breath. He let the breath out again, before saying, quietly, 'I've asked Sara if she'd like to—'

'But you *can't*!' Her face crumpled, and furiously she dashed a tear away. 'You can't marry again. You know you can't. You know you'll never fall in love, ever again. Not after Mom!'

Logan drew her into his arms just as she broke down and started sobbing.

'Sweetie—' he stroked her hair '—you're right. I'll never fall in love again. But there's something you don't know.' He tilted up her chin, and looked into her tear-filled eyes. 'You see, I have a secret…one I've never told anybody else in the world…'

Her weeping was diminishing, and when it ended in a hiccuping little sob he said softly, 'Before your mom died, she begged me to promise her that one day I'd marry again.'

He felt her thin body stiffen with shock. Her expression, as she responded to what he'd told her, was hard with censure. 'You didn't *have* to promise!'

'Honey, the way things were I'd have promised your mom the world if I could have given her it.'

Silence thrummed between them for a long, tense moment. Then Andy broke it.

'Why'd she want you to marry again?' she asked belligerently.

'Lots of reasons.'

'Not so I would have another mom! If that's the reason, then you can forget it! I don't *want*—'

'Andy, it was between your mom and me. Nobody else. Sweetie, some things you aren't going to understand until you're an adult but I'm asking you to trust me on this. You know how important it is never to break a promise. Have I ever broken a promise to you?'

She bit her lip. But she shook her head.

'Would you want me to break a promise to your mom?'

'No—' her voice wobbled '—of course not.'

'It's five years since she died. Five years since I made that promise, and I can't live with myself if I don't do something about it. I like Sara. And I think you like her too. We can all get along together. And nothing need change between you and me. You'll always be my special girl.' He kissed her brow. Held her shoulders and looked deep into her eyes. 'I think you'll be happy about the idea, once you get used to it. Hey!' He smiled ruefully. 'Maybe we don't even need to be having this conversation! Maybe Sara won't accept my proposal!'

'Turn you *down*?' Andy's tone was outraged. It seemed as if her objections to his taking a wife had been totally wiped out by the very idea that Sara—or any other woman!—wouldn't consider him the catch of the century! 'Daddy, if she turns you down, she'd have to be *out of her mind*!'

Out of her mind.

That was what she'd have to be, Sara reflected wryly as she drove her Toyota along West Vancouver's Marine Drive that evening, if she even spent one moment considering Logan's marriage proposal seriously.

Yet…she'd thought of nothing else all day.

She pulled off the street, into the parking area adjoining the Hunter West local office. After switching off the engine, she got out of the car, her thoughts winging back to the message she'd found on her answering machine when she'd come home from the store after work:

'I'm calling from West Van, Sara. I've had an offer on the island property, and at the moment counter-offers are flying back and forth like so much shrapnel, and I need to be on the spot in case something gels. We may have to put off our date till tomorrow...unless you care to drive over here, in which case we could grab a bite at Caper's; it's a stone's throw from the office. Call me at this number...'

So here she was. But she was early. She had time for a walk before meeting Logan, as arranged, in his office.

The breeze, warm and ocean-tanged, flirted with the hem of her cotton skirt as she strolled down 25th Street. A small fountain bubbled, in the centre of a half-moon seating area, and ahead lay the water, greyed, on this late summer evening, like the hazy sky.

She decided to walk out to the pier.

She was passing the picnic area when she saw them.

Travis and Tracy...and their son.

She might not even have noticed them, had the child not screamed. The sound drew her attention; she glanced over.

And froze.

For a solid moment, she froze, while the tableau branded itself on her brain, and she knew, with despair, that the image would remain burned there, for ever.

Travis. Immaculately dressed in a French navy business suit, light shirt, red tie. Looking as if he wanted to be anywhere but where he was.

Tracy. Sharp-featured Tracy. Red-haired Tracy.

Adul-
terous little Tracy. Hissing at their child, pulling him by
the arm.

And the child. Four years old. Dressed in designer
togs. Rigid on the grass. Screaming blue murder.

Sara's throat felt tight, as if someone was choking her.
Her heart seemed to be lurching drunkenly against her
ribs, banging, banging. Oh, God, oh, dear God, it was
the first time she'd ever seen Travis and Tracy together.

And the first time she had ever seen Travis's son.

She fought back a sob. She had to get out of there,
before—

She spun round and started walking back the way
she'd come. Forcing her legs to move. Telling her heart
to slow down. Telling her stomach to please keep its
contents, telling her eyes to squeeze back the tears...

The slope was steep and her calves began to ache.

But that ache was nothing compared with the pain in
her heart.

She made it back to her car before she broke down.
And then the tears came rolling, and with her arms bent
over the steering wheel, and her head bent over her arms,
she gave way to her misery.

She wasn't sure how long she wept.

When she finally gathered herself together, she took
in a quavering breath and set to, to repair the ravages
on her face. Using the rear-view mirror to check her
appearance, she applied more make-up to camouflage
the damage, taking time to brush a concealing layer of
blue shadow over the red rims of her eyes.

There was nothing she could do about the unhappiness
in the eyes themselves.

She had told Logan she didn't want to talk about

Travis's other betrayal. The betrayal that had almost destroyed her. Now she forced herself to think about it.

While married to her, while denying her the child she'd so desperately wanted, Travis had fathered another woman's baby.

The knowledge of that betrayal would haunt her to the end of her days.

When he'd discovered he'd been found out, Travis had tried, blusteringly, to explain himself to her.

Pregnancy, he'd told her, would have marred the perfection of her figure—thickened her waist, slackened her breasts, perhaps even striated her belly with stretch marks. Only then had she realised that to him she'd never been more than just an item in his collection of beautiful artifacts.

Hurt beyond belief, Sara had left him…and had sworn never to marry again, even knowing that the price she'd pay for that decision would be unbearably high.

She would never have a child, and a baby was something she longed for, more than anything else in the world.

'Another cup of coffee, Sara?'

'No, thanks.'

'Right.' Logan looked up at the waitress hovering by their window table. 'We'll have the bill, then, please.'

The waitress left, and Logan frowned as he looked at Sara. She was staring out over the ocean…and she might as well have been out there, halfway to Japan, as far as he was concerned.

She'd been late; he'd been standing at the street door of his office waiting for her when she'd turned up.

They'd come straight to the restaurant, where he'd booked a table.

He'd sensed a tension in her from the moment she'd hurried up, apologising for her lateness.

'Bridge traffic busy?' he'd asked.

She'd murmured something noncommittal.

And over dinner she'd been distant. They'd barely talked. He'd got the distinct feeling that she didn't want to be there. Had his proposal distressed her? Was she going to tell him, after dinner, that she didn't want to see him again? Was she going to give him the brush-off?

The thought depressed him indescribably.

After he'd paid the bill, they walked out to the street together.

'Let's go to the office,' he said. 'You're not in any hurry to get home, are you?'

'No. And I'm sure you're anxious to hear about your property sale.'

'I have my pager,' he said. 'If anything had happened, my secretary would have beeped me.'

As they walked down 25th, the tension emanating from her became electric; he could almost feel his hair stand on end. But once they'd turned left onto Bellevue she seemed to relax a little.

In the office, he introduced her to the senior secretary, Gladys.

'No word from the Rosscoes' lawyer yet, Mr Hunter,' Gladys said.

'Let me know when he calls. Mrs Wynter and I'll be in here.'

Logan opened a door, and led Sara into a small inter-view office. Sparsely furnished, it was one of several used for private consultations between agents and clients. Four cushioned chairs were set neatly around a low table.

He pulled out a chair for Sara, and she sat down.

He sat directly across from her.

'We have to talk,' he said. 'About my proposal.'

Sara looked across the round table at Logan.

How dear he had become to her.

And how she hated to turn him down.

Steeling herself, she formulated the words that were destined to do just that, because no way could she marry this man.

No woman in her right mind would marry a man who was still in love with his first wife.

She twined her hands together on the table, and saw the knuckles become white. She also saw, in her mind's eye, the scene that had so devastated her before she'd fled in tears from the beach area.

Travis…and his child.

If she married Logan, she could have a child.

The thought came out of nowhere. And it was so staggering, and so unexpected, she almost gasped.

She repeated it again, in her mind.

Deliberately.

If she married Logan, she could have a child.

A child she would love…and a child who would love her. Logan liked children…she knew that, by the way he was around his own daughter. He was the perfect father.

He would be the perfect father for her baby.

'Sara?' Logan's voice was puzzled. 'What is it?'

Sara blinked. She looked at Logan again, but this time

with different eyes. She no longer looked at him as a man who would never fall in love with her, but as the man who held the key to her most cherished dream.

'S-sorry,' she found herself stammering. 'What?'

He reached over and clasped her clenched fingers.

'Sara, dear—' his voice was quiet '—will you do me the honour of becoming my wife?'

The answer was trembling on her lips. Through a blur of sudden tears, she stared with a feeling of desperation at his kind face, his warm eyes, his beautiful lips... slanted in a smile that now held more than a hint of uncertainty.

'You've...talked with Andy?' Her heart was shaking. What was she thinking of? Was she *really* going to do this? Thank heavens she was sitting down; she felt weaker than a newborn kitten.

'Yes, we've talked. She...understands.'

Sara took in a deep breath and made her decision. And prayed it would turn out to be the right one.

'Then...I do, Logan. I do accept your pr—'

She didn't get the chance to finish. He'd pushed back his chair the moment she'd said 'I do'. He'd rounded the small table, and hauled her up into his arms.

He pulled her so close to him, he slammed the breath from her lungs. 'Thank God!' He kissed her with a passion that buckled her knees. After a startled moment, she caught her breath and kissed him back, returning passion for passion in a kiss so heated, she lost all sense of time and place.

He didn't love her, she thought giddily, but he certainly wanted her...every bit as much as she wanted him!

The kiss might have gone on for ever, had the office door not been opened from outside after a brisk knock.

'Mr Hunter, the Rosscoes—oops, sorry! I didn't realise…'

Logan turned, his arms still around Sara.

'Yes, Gladys?' he said, as smoothly as if his secretary had come upon him filling in forms. 'You were saying?'

Gladys's face was the colour of flame. 'The Rosscoes' lawyer just called; they won't meet your price. They've come back with a counter-offer. Fifty thousand less. If you ask me,' she said stoutly, 'it's an insult!'

'It's such a beautiful property,' Sara murmured. 'What a pity you're selling. Do you really *have* to?'

Following her comment came silence.

She felt Logan looking at her.

After a moment, he said, 'Gladys, would you mind…?'

Gladys said, 'Not at all,' and went out.

Logan's eyes were dark. 'What are you saying, Sara?'

'You've never really wanted to sell your summer place, have you?'

He frowned. 'Sara, the only reason I put it up for sale was because I knew it was time to get on with my life. My marriage to Bethany—it was all tied up with that house.'

'But in your heart you didn't want to sell. You still don't want to sell. And Andy…she loves it too.'

'Yeah, but—'

'Take it off the market. Can you do that, at this stage?'

'Well, sure I can, but—'

'Logan,' she said softly, 'just because you've decided to go forward, that doesn't mean you have to close every door behind you.'

He shook his head, and the expression in his eyes was so tender, she could scarcely bear the happiness sprinkling over her like stardust.

'You really are something else, Sara Wynter,' he murmured. 'But not for much longer...'

She quirked a questioning brow.

'Because in a short space of time,' he said, with a bone-melting smile, 'you'll be Mrs Logan Alexander Hunter.'

Logan was true to his word.

He took the property off the market.

But it was only with reluctance that he agreed to Sara's request that they delay the wedding till December. She wanted, in the meantime, to give her full attention to getting her store ready for opening. And later to fixing the teething troubles that would undoubtedly occur in the first few weeks of its operation.

So they decided on a Christmas Eve wedding...

A quiet civil ceremony, with Andy as Sara's attendant.

But, even as Sara looked forward to it, a black cloud hung over her.

Since the wedding announcement, Andy's attitude towards her had changed. The teenager had taken to sniping at her, but was careful to act that way only when Logan wasn't around. In addition, she avoided Sara where possible, and turned down every attempt on Sara's part to coax her back into their former friendly relationship.

So it was with some surprise that Sara saw Andy and Chrissie come into the store, on the afternoon before her 'grand opening'.

She'd been up on a chair, pinning blown-up balloons

to the ceiling. As the door swung shut behind them, she jumped down.

'Hi, girls, what can I do for you?'

Andy sloped across the store, the short checked skirt of her school uniform swinging above her knees. 'Nothing.' She lifted her thin shoulders in a careless shrug. 'Chrissie wanted to see the store.'

'So...what do you think of it, Chrissie?' Sara asked with a smile.

Sliding her hands into the pockets of her burgundy blazer, Chrissie looked around interestedly. 'It's, like, *really* nice, Mrs Wynter. My mom has a Sally Cole sweater; it's white with bluebirds on the pockets...'

'Oh, yes. One of my own favourites,' Sara said.

'She says she'll buy me a Sally Cole for my next birthday. She sometimes lets me wear her bluebird one. But not very often. Andy says you're going to invite me to your wedding. That's way cool—'

'Why aren't you inviting tons of *your* friends to the wedding, Sara?' Flippantly, Andy ran her hand over the skirt of the burnt-orange sweater dress adorning one of the store's two mannequins. 'Don't you have any?'

'When I get married,' Chrissie put in blithely, 'I'm going to invite all the girls I went to school with. It's going to be a blast!'

Sara moved over to the counter, and slipped up onto the high stool behind it. She folded her arms and leaned on the countertop, her thoughts turning over swiftly as she tried to decide what to say.

She wasn't about to reveal to these schoolgirls that her first husband had squeezed all her old friends out of her life. They were of a different generation; they wouldn't understand how any woman could allow herself to become such a doormat...

'Big weddings can be fun, Chrissie,' she said lightly. 'Planning them can also be a major headache. Right now, with the store, I have more than enough on my plate. Besides—' she glanced at Andy '—this is a second marriage for your dad and me...we both wanted something low-key.'

'Well, yeah,' Andy said, 'I can see why you wouldn't want the long white dress and all that fairy-tale stuff.' She threw Chrissie a sidelong look and gave a faint snicker. 'It's not like you're some *virgin bride* or anything!'

Ouch! Sara hid a wince at the open jab. Chrissie was looking uncomfortable, but Andy's eyes had a smug glitter as she fixed them challengingly on her future stepmother.

'You're right, Andy,' Sara said in a purposely casual tone. 'A fairy-tale white wedding is a once-in-a-lifetime event. It's something very special. The first time I got married, though, I did have the dreamiest white dress, silk and lace, with—'

'Let's go.' Andy took Chrissie's arm and pulled her towards the door. 'Mrs P. said she was going to make Belgian chocolate brownies this afternoon. I'm just starving.'

Although Chrissie flushed crimson and threw Sara an apologetic look, Andy didn't even glance at Sara as they left, and she slammed the door so hard, the glass shelves shuddered.

As did Sara.

She slumped down on her stool.

She could only guess at the pain Andy was feeling,

pain because she felt her mother's place was going to be taken by someone else. And pain because till now she'd had her father all to herself. It was understandable she'd feel grief, and resentment. But that was no excuse for rudeness. Sara hadn't wanted to call her on it, though—not in front of Chrissie.

She shook her head helplessly. It seemed the only way Andy knew to cope with her pain was to fight; but her sniping was nasty, and sly.

Sara hadn't mentioned the problem to Logan. She knew he'd insist on having it out with his daughter, which would only make matters worse—and make the unhappy teenager resent her future stepmother even more than she already did.

No, Sara had decided, this was something she and Andy had to sort out themselves.

The question was, how?

No matter how many times she asked herself the question, she was unable to come up with an answer!

CHAPTER ELEVEN

A RUSSET maple leaf drifted down in front of Sara as she walked up the path to Marla Craven's front door that evening.

How many times in the distant past had she walked up these steps? Sara wondered. Hundreds. Yet tonight, for the first time ever, she was nervous, unsure of her welcome.

The sensation was not a pleasant one. It clenched her stomach muscles, slicked her palms, made her want to run.

She lifted the heavy brass knocker, banged it hard once, then once again, and let it drop.

She counted to thirty before she heard approaching steps. She heard the steps pause; her pulse quickened as she imagined the other woman checking through the peephole.

The door swung slowly open.

Marla was wearing an emerald-green dress that set off her tall, slender figure, and her long ebony hair was twisted over one shoulder in a glossy hank. Her eyes, silver-blue and dark-lashed, were wary as they fixed on Sara.

She said no word of greeting. Just waited for Sara to speak.

But Sara found she couldn't. The words she'd meant to say, the words she'd planned so carefully, couldn't climb over the huge painful lump that had risen in her throat.

Tears pricked, and she blinked them back desperately. She swallowed, swallowed again, and finally managed to push the words out.

But when they emerged they weren't the ones she had planned: Travis and I are divorced. I'm on my own again, and I'd like to explain, ask you to forgive me...

What came out, in a rush and stumble, was, 'Oh, Marla, I've missed you so much...I've missed you so much...'

She'd been determined not to cry—and might have succeeded had she not seen the tears suddenly welling up in the other woman's silver-blue eyes.

Then she and her old friend were in each other's arms, hugging, weeping, babbling, making no sense whatsoever. Marla drew her inside, closed the door, and soothed her as if she were a small child needing comfort.

And only later, after they'd shared a pot of iced tea in Marla's solarium, and they had both dried their eyes and were actually managing watery smiles, was Sara able to explain to Marla why she had let their friendship lapse.

'We often used to wonder,' Marla said, sitting back in her cushioned wicker chair, 'Jane and Steph and I, what we'd done to offend you; we just couldn't figure it out...'

'Do you still meet for brunch every Sunday?'

'Oh, sure. Same time. Same place—' She broke off, a mischievous light suddenly glinting in her eyes. 'Are you free this Sunday?'

'Yes...I think so...as far as I know.'

Marla chuckled. 'Then let's surprise the others. How about if you turn up...just as if you'd never been away?'

'I'll look forward to it! It'll be lovely to see Jane and Steph again!'

Sara stayed for another hour, while she and Marla got caught up on all their news. Then Marla took her upstairs to see her five-year-old twins, Rob and Jake, who were sound asleep in their beds, a black Labrador dozing in a basket nearby.

'Dan's away on a business trip,' Marla murmured as she shut the bedroom door. 'He'll be so pleased to see you again. He always had a soft spot for you.' She grimaced. 'Travis—well, he was never one of Dan's favourite people.'

Before Sara left, she told Marla she'd have her round soon to meet Logan.

'And his daughter,' she added. 'It's thanks to Andy, really, that I decided to screw up my courage and come here tonight. She...just reminded me of how very much I need to have my old friends in my life.'

'And this time—' Marla hugged her tight '—you'll never get rid of us again!'

In the middle of the night, it rained. Sara had been in a light sleep, and the sound disturbed her. She got up and looked out of the window, and felt a pang of disappointment. This wet weather, if it continued, wouldn't encourage people to come to the opening of her store in the morning!

But when she woke next day it was to find that the rainstorm had passed, and the sun was shining.

She ate breakfast on the run—coffee and a bagel—

and when Logan called to pick her up, as arranged, she was almost ready.

She opened the apartment door and let him in. He kissed her, and then held her away from him.

'You're looking snazzy!' he said. 'And of course that's a Sally Cole outfit you're wearing?'

'What else?' She laughed, and looked down at the lightweight alpaca sweater dress. 'I just hope it's not going to be too hot—'

'Uh-uh.' He shook his head. 'There's a cool breeze this morning. Definite hint of fall in the air.'

But there was nothing cool in his gaze; his eyes were warm, and as she looked up into them she detected a darkening in the green colour.

'I have a present for you,' he murmured. 'Close your eyes.'

Sara obeyed.

She felt him take her left hand, but a moment later, when she realised what he was doing, her heart gave a great lurch and she opened her eyes.

In time to see him slide an engagement ring on her finger.

'This ring,' Logan murmured as he slid it over her narrow knuckle, 'will remain there for ever.' He raised her hand to his lips, and kissed her fingertips. 'As you and I shall remain together for ever.'

Tears shimmered in Sara's eyes, blurring her gaze as she looked at the sparkling sapphire. 'It's…it's just…oh, so beautiful, Logan.'

She raised her eyes to his, and he kissed her again.

'You like it?' he asked huskily. 'I wanted to surprise you…'

'I love it,' she whispered. *Just as I love you.* But she

didn't say the words. She didn't want to spoil the moment.

'Good.' He took her hand in his and held it firmly. 'So...let's get this show on the road,' he said. 'The grand opening of the Sally Cole boutique!'

Such a day!

And such a success.

At five-thirty, Sara saw her last customer out, locked the shop door, and exhaustedly walked over to the counter. Stumbling behind it, she hitched her behind up on the tall stool, and opened the till.

She had just finished sorting the money and locking it in the small built-in safe, when she heard a firm knock-knock on the back door.

Logan.

Gathering up her purse and the gift-bag she'd packed earlier, she crossed to open up the back door for him.

For *them.*

He'd brought Andy with him.

Sara's heart sank, but she managed a welcoming smile that included them both.

'Hi,' she said. 'You're right on time. I'll just lock this door and we can be on our way.'

As they walked to his Mercedes, Logan put his hand in the small of her back; Andy walked along on the other side of him. The teenager dived into the back seat of the car, and Logan opened the front passenger door for Sara.

'So...' He held the edge of the door and looked down at her as she settled her purse on the floor, and the gift-bag on her lap. 'How was it?'

Sara grimaced. 'Busy—but I'm certainly not complaining! I sold several pieces and got so many custom orders, I'm going to have to find two more knitters.'

'Wonderful!'

Logan closed the door, and as he rounded the bonnet Sara turned to Andy.

'I was hoping you'd come by, after school,' she said. 'I guess you were too busy.'

'Oh, yeah, I was real busy.' Andy stared stonily at her. 'I had to watch Oprah. It was a special programme on kids that get stuck with stepmothers.'

Sara felt a twinge of temper, and told herself to cool it. 'Andy—'

'*What?*'

'This is for you.' She dropped the gift-bag on the back seat.

It contained a sweater she'd designed while she'd been on the island, during those lovely peaceful afternoons she'd spent at the waterfall...before Logan had trespassed on her privacy. She'd knitted it herself, had been working on it for the past couple of weeks, whenever she had a moment. Made of heavy knit white cotton, it had a picture, on the back, of the summer place on Madronna Island.

Logan opened the driver's door and lowered himself into the seat.

Sara grasped her hands together on her lap, and tried to relax; but it was difficult. She could almost feel the hostile vibes coming from behind.

'I guessed,' Logan said, 'that you'd be tired, so I cancelled our reservation at the Pan Pacific and asked Mrs P. to cook us a special dinner. OK?'

Sara met his eyes as he glanced over at her, and she smiled. 'Sounds good to me,' she said.

And when he put his hand briefly on her knee and smiled back at her she felt her heart glow.

They were going to be happy together, she mused. Very happy together.

As for Andy...well, she was a fly in the ointment; there was no getting away from it. But Sara reassured herself that eventually, somehow, she'd find a way to get around her.

In the meantime, though she cocked her head to the side and listened, she heard no sound of paper rustling.

Andy might have desperately wanted her own Sally Cole sweater, just as Chrissie did. But she would, apparently, rather be hauled over white-hot coals than let Sara know it!

During the next few weeks, Sara didn't have much time to worry about her future stepdaughter.

The timing of her store-opening couldn't have been better. Fall was here, and women wanted sweaters. Pretty sweaters. Feminine sweaters. And sweaters designed to suit their own lifestyles, not sweaters churned out by the hundreds with clones available in every chain store.

They wanted Sally Coles—and Sara was happy to oblige.

She hired four new knitters, and soon found herself so busy in the store she had little time to do any knitting herself. But she didn't mind. Business was booming. She hired a middle-aged woman to help at the counter...

And what spare time she did have she used in making preparations for her wedding.

She had also resumed the Sunday brunches with her three old friends, and had taken Logan with her on one occasion, so they could meet him. He was an instant hit; and it worked both ways. Before brunch was over, he'd invited them to the wedding. Along with their husbands. And all their children. Sara's heart had glowed as she'd watched him interact so naturally with these women who meant so much to her.

'What a hunk!' Marla had rolled her eyes at Sara when the two women were alone in the powder room. 'And whatever's going on between the pair of you...the air's positively sizzling with it! Hot stuff, is he, my love?'

Sara had blushed, and laughed the comments off. But she knew what Marla meant. What Marla didn't know was that she and Logan weren't sleeping together.

They'd talked about it, in view of Andy's reaction to Logan's sleeping over at Sara's that one night...and had made a joint decision not to have sex again till after they were married.

It was driving Sara crazy!

And by the end of November she wondered if either of them could stand it much longer. She just needed to see Logan come into the store, or wandering around her apartment, or looking at her across a dinner table, and she was almost overcome with longing.

As for Andy...she didn't see much of her at all.

The teenager had never acknowledged the gift Sara had given her, and Sara, despairing of that breakthrough she'd been so fervently hoping for, finally began to lose heart.

Maybe, she decided, the situation would never be resolved.

*   *   *

December arrived, bringing with it crisp clear days and a growing closeness in Sara's relationship with Logan.

He'd taken to calling her every morning at work, but on the first Monday of the month he called her at home, around nine-thirty.

'Honey, are you all right?' His voice was concerned. 'I talked to Barbara and she said you hadn't come in yet, that you'd called to say you'd be late.'

'I'm just getting ready to leave.' Sara, hunched over on the edge of the mattress, had the receiver tucked between her ear and her shoulder as she pulled on a pair of wispy stockings. 'I was feeling a bit off when I got up...something I ate, more than likely...but I feel a lot better now.'

She caught sight of her reflection in the dressing-table mirror and frowned at her unhealthy pallor—a shade somewhere between pale grey and leaf-green. Ye gods, what had she eaten to make her look that way? Or had she picked up some bug from a customer in the store? 'Oh, damn!'

'What is it? Sara? Are you still there?'

Her laugh was wry. 'I just stuck my fingers through a fifteen-dollar pair of pantihose! Monday mornings,' she said as she got to her feet, 'should be outlawed!'

Logan said something, but she didn't catch what; she'd just been assailed by a wave of nausea. Bile rose in her throat, and she clutched a hand to her neck.

'Logan,' she said hurriedly, 'thanks for calling. I'm going to get dressed now...I don't want to leave Barbara coping in the store alone. Call you later!'

She hung up. And ran.

She got to the bathroom just in time, before she vomited.

* * *

Why did I ever rent a store next to a hamburger joint?'
Sara pressed a hand to her stomach as she and Barbara
left work shortly after five-thirty that day. 'I was feeling
better by the time I got here this morning, but that smell
of frying food...' It was making her faintly queasy again.

'Are you OK?' The older woman's round face
screwed up anxiously, making her bright blue eyes almost disappear. 'Honey, you've been looking wishy-
washy all day...'

'I guess I must be coming down with flu. If I'm no
better tomorrow, would you manage...on your own?'

'Oh, sure.' The sun glinted on Barbara's permed grey
hair as she walked her employer over to her car. 'But I
hope you don't mind if I... I was just wondering...'

Sara paused, her fingers curved around the handle of
the Toyota's door, her stomach tilting up and down and
sideways. 'Wondering what, Barbara?'

'I hope I'm not treading on tender tootsies,' the older
woman said hesitantly, 'but...is there any chance, dear,
that you might be pregnant?'

'Pregnant?' Sara echoed, feeling as if her legs were
going to give way under her. *Pregnant?*

Barbara touched her arm. 'Buy yourself a pregnancy
testing kit on your way home, dear. That way you can
find out tonight.'

With that, Barbara bustled her stout figure across to
her own car—a late-model white Honda.

Leaving Sara leaning back against her Toyota, gasping for breath, blinded by the sun, and as stunned with
shock as if she'd just been slammed into by a runaway bus!

Logan had been worried about Sara all day...ever
since she'd broken off their phone call so hurriedly
that morning...

But he'd been so busy he'd not been able to get away from the office...until now.

He paced back and forth, back and forth on the pavement outside her apartment building. Waiting. Frustratedly.

She was always regular as clockwork. Home here before six. It was now ten after—

He turned his head sharply as he heard the sound of a car engine, and breathed out a sigh of relief when he saw her Toyota come around the corner.

He walked across to her parking spot, and was there to greet her when she got out of the car.

Relief surged through him as she walked towards him. Her cheeks were flushed pink, and her eyes had a bright sparkle.

'Hi!' Smiling, she walked into his open arms. 'This is a nice surprise. I thought we weren't seeing each other again till *tomorrow* night!'

'I've had a day from hell,' he said lightly, 'and I needed comfort.'

'You've come to the right place,' she assured him. 'Let's go up and you can tell me all about it.'

She prepared a chicken salad for dinner, and they ate at her small table, in a corner of the living room.

Logan found himself watching her, in a way he never had before. He'd been so concerned about her; he hadn't been able to get her out of his mind all day. It had thrown him off-balance, this feeling of intense anxiety.

She seemed quite unaware of his silent scrutiny. She'd undone her hair from its French braid when they'd come upstairs, and she'd gone into the bathroom to splash cold water on her face. Now he could see the dampness of water on her brow as she bent over her plate.

How sweet she was, how vulnerable.

Something stirred deep inside him—a feeling of protectiveness, affection, warmth. How lucky he was, he thought, to have found a woman like Sara.

She glanced up, her eyes cloudy as if her thoughts were a thousand miles away, but when she saw that he was paying no attention to his food, but was sitting back in his chair, looking at her, she blinked.

'What is it?' She touched a fingertip to one cheek. 'Is my face dirty? Barbara and I were unpacking crates of wool this afternoon; the packages came from France— they were really grimy.'

Logan shook his head. 'Your face isn't dirty, Sara. Your face is beautiful.' As was her voice. He loved to hear her speak; it was like listening to soothing music. 'So...tell me,' he murmured, 'more about this wool...'

She always looked surprised that he would be interested in what she did; even now, her eyes widened, and she hesitated, just a little, before going on.

'Well, you know I've had so many requests for specialty wools, I decided to stock them. I'm going to devote a section of the store to them...and to designer knitting patterns...my own, of course, but others too...'

As she spoke, she gestured with her left hand, and the engagement ring sparkled as it caught the light.

His ring. On her finger. For ever.

Logan felt dazed, as if the flashing movement of the gems was hypnotising him. He had to keep reminding himself that he was marrying again only because of his promise to Bethany. A promise he felt compelled to keep. Honour-bound to keep. What he was entering into with this woman was a marriage of convenience.

A contract.

A 'business merger'.

But, dammit, it just felt so right!

CHAPTER TWELVE

'SARA WYNTER! What are *you* doing here?'

With a guilty start, Sara whirled round from the display of diapers she'd been studying...to find her friend Marla right behind her, her eyes wide and speculative.

'Oh, hi, Marla.' Darn it! Sara wished, too late, that she had stayed home this Thursday evening, instead of hying herself down to the Bay, where she'd been inexorably drawn to the baby department. 'I'm...er...'

Marla's mouth fell open. 'Good grief!' she cried. 'You're pregnant!'

Several shoppers turned to stare, and Sara grimaced.

'Hush!' She snatched Marla's arm and pulled her behind a stand of yellow blankets. 'For heaven's sake, keep your voice down!'

'But it's wonderful!' Marla hugged her so hard, Sara thought her ribs would surely crack. 'Logan must be over the moon!'

'Marla.' Sara shook her head, torn between frustration and affection and the tears that seemed to come all too readily these days. 'Logan doesn't know. Not yet.'

Marla did a double take. 'Well, when are you going to tell him?'

'He's taking me to a concert at Andy's school tomorrow night. I'm going to break the news afterwards. I did the pregnancy test on Monday night but I wanted to be absolutely sure there was no mistake. So I waited. My doctor confirmed it today.' She shook her head ruefully.

'I can't believe I didn't even notice what was happening.'

'It's not too surprising; you've been so busy, what with all the excitement of your engagement, and the store opening, and making all your wedding plans…'

'I guess. Anyhow, I *was* planning to call you soon, but of course I wanted Logan to be the first to know.'

'And his daughter,' Marla said. 'She'll be pleased, I imagine, to have a brother or sister. A girl that age, the mothering instinct's already kicking in, isn't it?'

Sara fervently hoped that this would be so, and that the coming baby would be the key to opening Andy's heart. But she'd never discussed Andy's hostile attitude with Marla, so all she said now was, 'I'm sure you're right. But what are *you* doing here? Don't tell me *you're* pregnant!'

Her friend chuckled. 'No way. The two I have keep me on the hop—I couldn't cope with a third. But my sister-in-law…you remember Jamie?…she's going to have a baby next month. I came by to look for a gift. Now, Sara, be sure to call me and let me know what that yummy husband of yours says when you tell him he's going to be a daddy!'

The concert was a musical one, and Andy was in the choir.

Sara and Logan sat in the third row from the front, and throughout the two hours the show lasted he had his arm draped over the back of her seat.

She was unbearably aware of his closeness all evening, and by the time the show was over she could think of nothing but being alone with him.

As they left the hall and went out into the dusk to

wait for Andy, he took her hand in his. The contact sent sizzles of wanting through her till she felt she might pass out with the excitement of it.

People milled around them in the car park; he ignored them all. Leaning back against his car and looping his arms around her, in that way so familiar to her now, he pulled her close. 'I don't know,' he said huskily, 'if I can wait till after we're married before we—'

'But...we agreed it would be for the best.' A blush heated her cheeks.

'A mistake. And one I intend to rectify. All evening I've been able to think of nothing else but going to bed with you.' He pulled her tighter, and through her light suit she was made well aware of just how much he wanted her. 'Sara, I want you so much, I ache—'

'Dad!' Andy's voice interrupted him. 'Ready?'

Logan's breath hissed in sharply. 'Ready as I'll ever be!' he whispered to Sara before releasing her.

They both turned, to see Andy coming towards them.

'Hi, Sara,' she said. 'Did you enjoy the concert?'

Andy was putting on what Sara now thought of as 'her act'. Pleasant, polite, friendly...when her father was around!

'It was lovely,' Sara said.

'Thanks so much for coming with Dad,' Andy added as Logan opened the car doors. 'I really appreciate it!'

Her words and tone were amicable, but were belied by the taunting glitter in her eyes. Sara felt her happiness dull. Perhaps she'd have to talk to Logan about Andy's attitude, after all. Unless, of course, the news about the coming baby did bring about a happy change in her behaviour.

But first of all she had to tell Logan she was going to have his child.

And she would do that in her own apartment, after he'd driven her home.

She couldn't wait!

'Pregnant?' Logan stared at her, his green eyes stark with shock and disbelief. 'How the hell did *that* happen?'

Sara froze. The only part of her able to move was her mind, and it was reeling in dismay. Of all the reactions she'd envisaged getting from Logan, anger had not been one of them.

'How did it happen?' She glared right back at him. 'The way these things usually happen, of course! We did make love, if you'll just cast your—'

'We had sex. We had it once. And I used—'

'Accidents happen.' But surely *this* wasn't happening? Surely she wasn't standing here, in her own living-room, with the father of her unborn baby glowering at her as if she'd committed the crime of the century? She closed her eyes. And the memory of how they'd been, earlier, made her want to weep. Where was it now, that rapport, that wanting, that—?

'For God's sake!' he snapped.

She opened her eyes, to see he'd started pacing the room. Restlessly. Distraughtly. He raked back his hair with both hands. Stopped. Glared at her some more.

'Well—' Sara spoke in a merry voice that she didn't recognise '—I can see that you're not exactly happy about this turn of events—'

'Damned right!'

Her heart felt like a lump of congealed lead.

'In that case,' she went on, in the same airy tone, 'we'd best call the wedding off. I intend to have the baby, and though I'd prefer to bring up the child with a father I'm perfectly capable of doing so alone.' She waited a blink, in the desperate expectation that she'd been totally wrong about his response, that somehow they'd got their wires crossed. But when he continued to inflict that black gaze on her that wink of expectation faded to nothing. And she felt, for the first time, the beginnings of her anger.

'I'd like you to leave now,' she said. And it was only with the greatest effort of self-control that she stopped herself from adding bitchily, At least Andy will be pleased that the wedding's off. I can tell you now that your daughter has been insufferably rude to me ever since we became engaged and I'd had just about as much of her as I could take.

Instead, she strode across the room, chin high, and held the door open for him.

'You know what's ironic?' she said in an icy tone. 'My ex-husband didn't want me to have a baby either, and that's what finally broke us up too! Oh, it wasn't that Travis didn't want a child—he had one with his mistress! You see, he didn't want me to have a baby because he was afraid I'd lose my youthful figure.' She curled her upper lip in a sneer. 'So...what's *your* excuse, Logan? What are *you* afraid of?'

Logan stared at her as if she'd just given him a death sentence. She felt a lurch of alarm as she noticed that all the colour had drained from his face. He looked ghastly.

Her own anger vanished as love kicked in again. She wanted to reach out to him, beg him to stay, tell him they could talk this out, make things work...somehow make things work.

But the expression in his eyes stopped her.

Those green eyes were as cold as the grave. And as forbidding.

He moved then, but it seemed just lifting his feet required a supreme effort. He walked past her. Without a word.

She didn't try to stop him.

And as she listened to his retreating steps she felt her heart break into a thousand pieces.

Next day, she jumped every time the phone rang.

But Logan didn't call.

In the evening, she knew she needn't expect to hear from him; he was going to be down in Seattle at an important conference.

It would be the perfect time, she decided, to go round to his place and return the ring.

She'd been so distressed by their confrontation, at the time she'd forgotten all about it. In movies, she knew, heroines threw the ring at the hero on occasions such as those; in her case, she'd been too upset to even think about doing such a thing.

On her arrival at his home, the housekeeper answered, on the intercom.

'It's Sara Wynter. May I come up?'

Mrs P. buzzed open the door, and as Sara ascended in the elevator she hoped Andy wouldn't be home.

It was the housekeeper who opened the condo door for her. 'Mr Hunter,' she told Sara, 'isn't here—'

'I know. I just want to go up to his bedroom and leave something for him. I'll let myself out...'

'Oh, sure.' The housekeeper disappeared in the direction of the kitchen.

Sara climbed the stairs, and went into Logan's bedroom.

The moment she did, she was assaulted by the familiar scent of his cologne, and her heart spiralled in despair.

She took the ring from her finger, and crossed to his tallboy, her high heels clicking on the parquet floor. Frowning, she looked for a place to leave the ring.

In the end, she set it inside a mahogany-lidded box where he kept his cufflinks.

Tears blurred her gaze as she left the room.

She had just reached the landing, and was about to descend the stairs, when she heard a door open behind her. Her pulses lurched.

'What are *you* doing here?' Andy's voice, insolent and harsh, came from behind.

Sara turned.

'I was just leaving something for your father—'

'He's in Seattle.'

'I know.'

The teenager swaggered forward, her expression mocking. 'So I can say what I like, without him hearing.'

'That's right.' Sara kept her voice steady. 'You can say anything you like. So why don't you? Why don't you get it right out of your system?'

She braced herself as the child came to a rigid stop in front of her, so close, Sara could smell the strawberry scent of her shampoo.

'I wish you'd butt right out of our lives,' Andy hissed. 'We don't want you, and my dad and I were just fine till you came along. You think he loves you? Huh! He's only getting married again because he promised my mom he would. Mom *made* him promise, before she died. He told me. And my dad always keeps his promises, no matter what…'

Sara flinched from the violent emotion in Andy's voice…and from her hurtful words.

She stumbled back as if the girl had struck her. The metal tips of her high heels were rough-edged and they caught on the looped carpet. She lost her balance. She started to fall. Backwards. She flailed desperately for something to hold onto. There was nothing. She cried out, the sound echoing in her ears as she tumbled into space.

She thought she heard Andy scream.

And after that…

Oblivion.

'I've lost my baby…'

With an anguished moan, Sara dug her face into the white pillow. A hospital pillow. Saturated with her tears.

She'd just wakened from a heavy sleep, and now she realised that even while she'd slept she'd been weeping.

'I've lost my baby…' She couldn't seem to stop repeating the words. 'I've lost my baby…'

A sound at the doorway had her trying to catch the sobs choking her. She didn't want anyone to see her this way, so pathetically self-pitying, and drowned in misery. Swiping the hem of the sheet over her eyes, she turned her head, and cast her blurred gaze to the door…

Andy. Standing in the doorway.

The child's face, as she stared at Sara, was ashen, her eyes stark with disbelief…and horror.

'You…were…*pregnant*?' She sounded as if she could barely get the words out.

Sara squeezed her eyelids closed, but the tears escaped anyway. Her lips felt parched. She ran her tongue over them, and tasted salt.

'Yes,' she whispered in despair. 'I was going to have a baby...'

For a long moment there was silence in the room. And then, from the doorway, came a cry like the cry of a wounded animal. A cry that found its echo in Sara's heart.

She drew in a quavering breath, tried to get a grip on herself, before opening her eyes again.

But when she did, when she looked across at the door, it was to find Andy had gone.

And someone else was coming in. A nurse. Red-haired and big-bosomed, with a cheery florid face.

'Well, now, Mrs Wynter...and what did you say to upset your young visitor?' The nurse whisked a thermometer from her pocket as she crossed the room. 'That poor girl, it's way past her bedtime, but no matter how her housekeeper tried to coax her to leave she just wouldn't go home till you wakened again and she could see you. So...what did you say to upset her?'

The nurse stood by the bed, and waited, her ginger brows raised in question.

Sara curled her fingers around the edge of the sheet. 'I told her...about...my baby.'

'What about your baby?' The other woman shook the thermometer.

Sara fought back a sob. Nurses had to cope with death on a daily basis; some folks said it made them hard. Sara had never thought so...till now. This nurse's grey gaze was merely curious. Not a single spark of compassion in sight.

'I told her,' Sara managed, over the huge lump in her throat, 'that I'd lost my baby.'

'Now why in tarnation would you have told her a lie like that?'

Sara stared. 'I lost my baby,' she said, her voice cracking. 'When I fell...'

'My dear Mrs Wynter—' the nurse slid the thermometer brusquely into Sara's mouth '—you did no such thing! And if you believe you did, then that crack on the head must have done more than just give you a mild concussion; it must have caused you to hallucinate. Or perhaps you just had a bad dream. At any rate, I can assure you your baby is fine—absolutely fine. The gynaecologist who examined you did remark that it would take more than a tumble down a flight of stairs to dislodge this particular infant!' She smiled, revealing deep dimples. 'That's something you might want to pass on to your young friend next time you see her!'

For a moment, Sara could do nothing but stare. Had she really dreamed it all, then—dreamed the coiling pain in her back, dreamed that headlong rush to the OR, dreamed the nightmare moment when that doctor, garbed in dark green, had told her, soberly, that she'd suffered a miscarriage?

Hysterical relief flowed through her, warming every cell in her body, and filling her heart to overflowing. She wanted to put her arms around the bosomy nurse, hug her tightly, apologise for her foolishness.

Instead, she closed her eyes, and sent up a profound prayer of thanks.

But even as she did she felt a vast emptiness in a corner of her heart. That corner where Logan had once

been. She still had her baby, and for that she would be
eternally grateful.

But her pregnancy had caused her to lose the man she
loved.

God, how he hated hospitals!

Goosebumps rose on Logan's skin as he strode along
the bare-walled, white-tiled corridor. He hated the
smells...the antiseptic, the floor polish, the sickness.

And the memory of death.

Bethany's death.

It was in this very hospital she had died.

Bile rose in his throat as images rose in his mind.

He didn't consider himself a coward, but if there was
one situation he wasn't...comfortable...in it was around
illness.

But here he was, now. And here was where he had to
be.

He'd been at a late evening meeting in Seattle when
Mrs P. had paged him. He'd left immediately, and it had
only been by a sheer miracle that he hadn't racked up a
dozen speeding tickets on the road north.

He'd come straight to the hospital.

At the nurses' station, they'd told him Mrs Wynter
had suffered a mild concussion but was just fine now;
and her baby, too, was just fine.

He'd had to lean against the desk to support himself,
and hadn't realised, till that second, just how *terrified*
he'd been of what he might hear.

'She's been drifting in and out of sleep,' a red-headed
nurse had told him, with a dimpling smile. 'So why don't
you just go along there, sit by the bed, and you'll be
there when she awakes again? Room 324.'

He reached the door. Swung it open, with the utmost care, and without making a sound.

The room was dimly lit, and though there were two beds only one was occupied.

The one over by the window.

Sara was asleep.

He closed the door silently, and stood there, looking at her. Her hair lay spread out on the pillow, the ends tangled, and her face was pale. Her lips were slightly parted, and he could see her chest rising and falling, in a regular rhythm.

The sheet was tucked over her breasts, and her arms lay over the white bedcover, the last of her summer tan showing brown, in contrast to the pale hospital gown and the—

Her hands were bare.

His ring was no longer on her finger.

Pain slashed his heart; when had she removed it? After the confrontation in her apartment?

Remorse swelled up inside till it almost choked him.

How could he have been so cruelly self-centred? How could he have allowed his personal demons to control his reactions? She'd told him she was expecting his child and all he could think of was Bethany. And his guilt. That damned corroding guilt over her death. Because, in the final analysis, he had been the one who had caused it—

'Logan?'

Sara was awake. Her voice, weak and threaded with surprise, broke into his tormented thoughts.

He crossed to her, quickly, and sat down on the chair by the bed.

She didn't move. Didn't reach out to him. Didn't smile.

Her eyes had a bottomless sadness that tore at him.

'Oh, honey,' he whispered. 'I'm so sorry.' He took her hands in his. They were cool, and lifeless. 'The last thing in the world I want to do is upset you. I have to explain, I need to explain, why I acted the way I did—' His voice caught. 'Darling, I want our baby, desperately want our baby—'

He gathered her up in his arms and held her close. She made a whimpering sound, and then he felt her arms go around his neck.

'Oh, Logan.' Her lips trembled against his neck as she whispered his name. 'I love you so much...'

Dismay rippled through her.

She hadn't intended to say that! She hadn't intended to confess her secret. But she couldn't take the words back.

How would Logan react to them? She felt as if her blood had stopped flowing; as if her whole body was on hold.

He slid his arms up to her shoulders, she heard his ragged intake of breath...and then—

'Mr Hunter!' The door was pushed open, the red-haired nurse rushed in, breathlessly. 'Phone call!'

She stood there, with the edge of the door in her hands.

Logan squeezed Sara's shoulders, his eyes met hers, and his were dark with emotion. 'Don't go anywhere,' he said softly. 'I'll be right back.'

He didn't come back.

The nurse did, a few minutes later.

'Mr Hunter has gone home,' she said. 'He asked me to tell you he'll get back to you just as soon as he possibly can.'

Sara lifted her head from the pillow, felt it begin to ache. 'What is it?' she asked. 'Is something wrong?'

'Oh, I'm sure not. It was his housekeeper. Mrs Pangoulis, or some such name.'

'What did she want?'

'Whatever it is, it's nothing for you to get upset about. You must think about your baby...worrying won't do him any good, will it? You just lie back, dear,' she said soothingly, 'and I'm going to bring you a nice basin of hot water so you can freshen up. Breakfast will be at eight and I'm sure your nice Mr Hunter will be back by then.'

He wasn't.

And when the doctor made his rounds at nine-thirty, and told Sara she was free to go, she dressed quickly, and checked out with minimum fuss and maximum speed.

She took a cab to Logan's condo, and told the cabbie to wait; she wasn't sure how long she'd be.

Mrs P. buzzed her up, and ushered her into the foyer. Sara felt a sharp pang of anxiety when she saw the deep worry lines on the housekeeper's forehead.

'It's Andy.' The older woman pressed a hand to her chest. 'She went to her room after we got home from the hospital, and I assumed she'd gone to sleep. About an hour later, I heard someone moving around and, thinking Mr Logan had come home, I got up. But it wasn't Mr Logan. That's when I went to check on

Andy.' Tears filled her eyes. 'And that's when I found…she'd run away.'

Sara felt as if the bottom had fallen out of her stomach. 'Run away?' she echoed in a rasping voice.

'I called the hospital, and Mr Hunter came right home. He's been out looking for her ever since. Me, I'd like to go out hunting for her myself, but somebody's got to stay here in case the little lamb comes home.'

'Where's Mr Hunter now?' Sara tried to control the panic rising up like a sword against her throat.

'He phoned just ten minutes ago,' the housekeeper said. 'From the police station. But they won't do anything yet, because the child's been missing for only a few hours.'

'I'm going home to get changed,' Sara said. 'Next time he calls in, please tell him to come by and pick me up—'

The phone rang. She froze.

The housekeeper rushed to the phone. She listened for a moment, and then said, 'I'll let you speak to Mr Hunter's fiancée. Mrs Wynter. She'd be the best person to speak to…Mr Hunter isn't home at present.'

Sara took the receiver. 'Hello, this is Mrs Wynter—'

'Mrs Wynter, this is Mavis Cornwell. My husband and I bought the old Hunter place, in Point Grey…'

Sara's heart sank. They must be having problems with their property. This was business. Nothing to do with Andy. 'Mrs Cornwell, could you call the Vancouver office? Mr Hunter's busy at present, but I'm sure one of his agents can—'

'Is he, by any chance, out looking for his daughter?'

For a moment, Sara couldn't speak. 'Well, yes,' she

finally managed. 'He is…but—how on earth did you know that?'

'She's here.' The caller had lowered her voice, as if afraid of being overheard.

'She's with *you*?'

'Well, not actually with us—'

'Then *where*?'

'She's in the garden. In what used to be…her mother's rose garden. There's a gazebo there. With cushioned seats. When my husband was leaving for work a few minutes ago, he noticed…'

'She was sleeping there?'

'Yes. Looked like she'd been there all night.'

'Is she…still out there?'

'Mmm.'

'Give me your address…I'll be right over.' Sara closed her eyes as the woman spoke, and memorised the address. 'Thank you so much, Mrs Cornwell, for phoning.'

She depressed the telephone plunger and thrust the handset at the housekeeper.

'Call Mr Hunter,' she said over her shoulder as she ran to the door. 'Tell him to meet me as soon as he possibly can at his old house in Point Grey.'

CHAPTER THIRTEEN

SARA'S feet made no sound as she walked across the lawn to the rose garden.

It was easy to find; the gazebo's turret was of shiny metal, and it glinted in the dull December sunshine.

But when she got closer she saw, with a heavy thudding of her heart, that the gazebo itself was empty.

She was about to turn away, when she heard a creaking sound.

She followed the rounded contours of the latticed arbour and on the other side she found the source of the sound—a child's swing, hanging on thin chains from the branch of an oak.

Sunshine stole through the tree's winter-bare branches, to glint on the brown hair of the girl listlessly moving the seat, toeing the ground below with the tips of her sneakers.

The sunshine also dappled the garment into which the girl was huddled, and it was with a profound sense of shock that Sara recognised the Sally Cole sweater she'd knitted for the teenager. What did it mean, that she was choosing to wear it now? Sara held her breath as hope swelled inside her.

She moved forward and a twig snapped under her foot.

Andy's head jerked up.

Her eyelids flickered when she saw Sara, but the eyes

themselves were devoid of expression, the rims red and swollen, her cheeks blotchy.

Sara felt the child's anguish as if it were her own.

For a long moment they just looked at each other, and then, without a word or even a smile of greeting, Sara walked in behind the swing, and, grasping the chains, pulled the swing back, and set it in motion.

For quite some time she continued to push, each time the swing came towards her.

And after a while Andy started pumping.

Apart from the chirping of birds in the garden, and the distant hum of traffic, the only sound was the rhythmic creak of the swing.

Until Andy finally spoke.

'It was my fault,' she said without intonation, 'that my mom and my baby sister died.'

Sara's breath jarred in her throat; it was only with the most supreme effort on her part that she managed to keep control of her actions. Without breaking her rhythm, she continued to push the swing.

'Tell me,' she said, 'all about that.'

She saw the child's small fingers tighten around the chains till the knuckles were butter-yellow.

'I didn't want anything to change. My mom and my dad and me. That's the way I liked it, and that's the way I wanted it to stay. For ever. But she...Mom...wanted to have another baby. And so...she got pregnant.'

Sara felt as if she was treading on eggshells as she said, 'And that made you...unhappy?'

'I wished it wasn't there.' Andy was no longer pumping; Sara had to push extra hard to keep the swing in motion. 'I heard her telling Dad she wanted it for me, so's I'd have a brother or a sister, and not be alone...but still I just kept on wishing, and wishing, that it wasn't true. I…prayed…that there would be no baby.'

Oh, God. Sara stared at the thin shoulders, slumped helplessly. At the small head, bowed low. 'Tell me,' she whispered.

But, with a gulping sob, the child leaped off the swing. She took off across the lawn, in the direction of the street.

Sara caught up with her inside the garden, right at the corner of a path lined with tall hedges. She grasped her arms, held her tight. 'What happened, Andy?'

No answer. Just a rasping moan.

With the fingers of one hand, she tipped the small face up. Forced it up. At sight of the child's ravaged expression, she felt a surge of nausea.

'Tell me,' she insisted. 'You have to tell me!'

'The baby died!' The confession came out in a thin wail. 'First the baby died, before it was born…and then my mom wasn't well and her heart gave out and she died…too…'

Oh, dear God.

Sara clasped the uncontrollably shuddering body to her breast and wondered how such a small child could have carried such an enormous, heart-crushing burden of guilt for so very long. And alone. For Sara knew, as surely as if Logan had been there to tell her, that Andy had never shared this secret sorrow with her father…or with anyone.

'Hush, darling.' She smoothed Andy's tousled hair. 'Hush. You must never think it was your fault. Lots of children think the kind of thoughts you were having; they're perfectly natural. Even if you'd never thought them, things would have turned out…exactly the way they did…'

'And then—' Andy's voice was muffled against Sara's chest '—then it all happened again. I wished you weren't there, I even told you I wanted you not to be there, and,' she sobbed, 'you ended up in hospital. But I never knew you were going to have a baby! And it's all happening again. You don't have a baby any more and it's all my fault…'

'Oh, Andy, you're wrong! I was wrong…about my baby. You see, I must have been having a bad dream, and that's when you came to my room, just after.' Her own voice caught in a half-sob, but there was a smile in it too. 'I didn't lose the baby, Andy. When I fell…it didn't hurt the baby…'

Andy raised a tear-stained face, shoved strands of wet hair from her eyes, and Sara saw that her gaze was filled with dawning hope, as if she'd seen a miracle and wanted to be reassured *she* hadn't been dreaming!

'A m-mistake?' she stammered. 'Are you sure? It's going to be all right? The baby…it's safe?'

'Yes.' Sara hugged her tight, and felt Andy's arms go round her waist and hug her back. 'Yes, sweetie, the baby's safe.'

Andy's blotchy cheeks slowly became totally suffused with colour. She bit her lip. 'Sara—' her voice was low '—I'm really sorry for the way I've been acting with you. So rude and…obnoxious. Dad's been so happy since he met you, and I guess I was…jealous. I *know* I don't deserve this—but could we start over again? You've always been so nice to me…and the worst of it—the thing that makes me feel more yukky than anything—is knowing that you never even told Dad about how—'

'Never told Dad what, young lady?'

Andy gasped; Sara felt her heart stand still. Then, together, they spun round.

Logan looked as if he'd been up all night. Which, of course, he had been. His jaw was darkly stubbled, his eyes bloodshot, his features strained. But even as he scowled at his daughter Sara could see the look of relief in his eyes.

'Oh, Dad…' With a gulping sob, Andy stumbled over to him, and he drew her into his arms.

'You're shivering,' he said quietly. 'Let's get you home and into a hot bath.'

Over Andy's head, his eyes met Sara's. 'As for you, Mrs Wynter, the last thing you should be doing in your present state is racing around looking for lost children. Once we get back to the condo—'

'I have a cab waiting, Logan.'

'Correction—you *had* a cab waiting.'

'But I hadn't paid the driver yet!'

'That's all taken care of.'

She opened her mouth to protest…and closed it again. Independence was all very well, but right now it felt good to have Logan taking care of things. She had to admit that now the emergency was over, and Andy was safe and sound, she herself was beginning to feel a bit wobbly.

And what was not helping the wobbly feeling was the anticipation of what lay ahead.

At the hospital, she'd confessed to Logan that she was in love with him. At the time, he hadn't been given the chance to respond…but he would, at the first opportunity. And she wasn't looking forward to it, because she knew he had proposed marriage to her only to fulfil his promise to his late wife. And she knew that whatever his response would be it would be the unvarnished truth…and she didn't know if she was woman enough to take it.

'Dad,' Andy said, 'I'd better go to the house and apologise to Mrs Cornwell for using her rose garden as a camping ground.'

'A good idea,' Logan said. 'We'll walk out to the car and meet you there. Say hi to the Cornwells for me.'

'OK, Dad.'

Logan watched her go, his eyes thoughtful.

'What is it, Logan?' Sara asked.

'Andy and I have always referred to it as her mother's rose garden,' he murmured. 'Did you notice, Sara, that just now Andy referred to it as Mrs Cornwell's rose garden?'

'Yes.' Sara smiled. 'Yes, Logan, I did notice.'

'I think—' he took her hand and pulled it against his thigh '—both my daughter and I have turned a corner this day.'

Logan smiled as Mrs P. greeted her young charge and fussed over her like the proverbial mother hen. Andy was hustled upstairs, and moments later Logan heard the faint sound of pipes humming as the housekeeper ran water for a bath.

He turned from staring out of the sitting-room window and fixed his gaze on Sara, who was reclining on a long couch.

'I'm not an invalid,' she'd protested when he'd suggested she lie down; but when he'd insisted she'd thrown him a rueful smile and given in gracefully as he'd placed pillows under her head and slipped off her shoes.

Now she was watching him, those turquoise eyes wary.

As well they might be.

There was much more to this little escapade than would seem on the surface. Of that he was positive.

He had no intention of distressing Sara if he could help it, but he meant to get to the bottom of whatever had been going on between his daughter and this woman he was going to marry.

'What was it,' he asked, 'that you never told me?'

He saw a nerve twitch below her right eye. 'It was something between the two of us. Between Andy and me. We've sorted it out now—don't ask Andy about it, Logan. Please.'

'Has she been giving you a hard time? Behind my—' He broke off, the involuntary flush rising on Sara's cheeks all the answer he needed. 'Dammit,' he snapped, 'I won't tolerate rudeness! I'll ground her till—'

'Logan…'

Her voice was quiet, but something in it sent a chill racing over his skin. 'What?'

Her face had paled again. 'Andy told me your wife died…' she swallowed '…having a baby.'

He scraped a hand agitatedly through his hair. 'I should have talked about that with you, Sara, but—'

'And your daughter blames herself, totally, for both their deaths.'

The chill icing Logan's skin seeped deep into his bones. 'No, that's not true.' He made a wild sweeping gesture with one hand. 'Not true at all. Andy had nothing whatsoever to do with it. Bethany had heart problems;

the doctors warned her not to have any more children, they told her, over and over and over, that the risk was too great—'

'Andy didn't want the baby.' Sara sat up, swung her legs over the edge of the sofa. 'She's been tortured by guilt ever since her mother died, because she believes her...bad wishes...were responsible for what happened.'

Logan couldn't have felt more sick had someone punched him in the gut. 'You're sure of this?'

Sara got to her feet. 'Absolutely.'

'My God. All this time. Five whole years. How could I have been so...blind?' Blood roared in his ears. 'That poor kid.' He turned from Sara, unable to bear the compassion—compassion and tears—shining in her eyes.

He walked to the window and stared out, his own gaze blurred.

'Logan—'

'It was my fault,' he said in an agonised tone, 'that Bethany died. No one else's.' He braced himself with a hand against the wall. 'She wanted another child so very badly, and I could refuse her nothing. She herself had been an only child. And a very lonely child. She was *determined* that Andy would never feel that kind of loneliness. She wanted her to have a sister...or a brother. And—' his voice broke '—she was prepared to risk her own life to—'

'But Logan, if it was what she *wanted*—'

He wheeled round. 'It was too dangerous! Don't you see? It was too dangerous! But because I was in love with her, because I could refuse her nothing, she died! I should never have given in!' His voice was raw with torment.

Sara ran to him. She threw her arms around him, and

pressed her cheek to his chest. He felt her tears wet his shirt.

'Oh, Logan,' she cried, 'you mustn't blame yourself any longer. All you were guilty of was trying to give Bethany her heart's desire.' She raised her face and looked up at him beseechingly. 'She chose to take that risk, and it was her right to make that decision. Don't you see? It wasn't *your* decision. It was *never* your decision to make.'

'But—'

'Don't torture yourself any longer, Logan. Do you think this is what Bethany would have wanted?'

He shook his head. 'It's the last thing she'd have wanted,' he said quietly. 'You're right. It *was* her decision to make. I don't know why I've never been able to see it that way.'

'Till now?'

He managed a smile. 'Till now. And I guess, in a way, I was being selfish. I wanted things to stay the same. In that regard, my motivations were similar to Andy's. We both liked our family exactly as it was. We didn't want anything that might screw it up...'

He slipped his fingers around the back of Sara's neck, caressed her cheeks with his thumbs.

'I'm going up to talk with Andy now,' he said. 'This may take some time. Will you stay?'

'No, I'll go home. I need to call Barbara—'

'You're not planning on going in today?'

'No, but I have to tell Barbara she's going to be on her own. I'll call a cab. And later...once you and Andy have talked...come and see me. I'll be waiting for you.'

It was close to lunchtime before Logan turned up.

He was wearing a leather jacket, and when Sara took

it from him she saw he was dressed in a charcoal-grey sweater and grey trousers. He'd shaved, and his eyes were clear. He looked relaxed…and, she thought, happy.

'Everything went well?' she asked as she hung up his jacket and closed the closet door.

'Yeah,' he said, 'we've cleared the air. Got pretty heavy, there, for a while…emotionally. There's a lot of depth to my daughter…much more so than I'd ever realised. By the way, I didn't have to ask her about her bad attitude to you; she offered that on her own. She's so sorry—'

'It's over, Logan.'

'She likes you.'

'I like her. She's easy to like.' Sara smiled. 'So's her dad!'

'Easy to like, Sara?' Logan took her left hand in both of his and held it loosely. 'Or…easy to love?'

His steady gaze demanded honesty.

'Yes.' She stared into his green eyes. 'Easy to love.'

'I didn't ask for your love.' He traced a fingertip round the mark where his ring had been. 'You said…that day we went sailing…that a marriage based on love was for fools…and the only kind of marriage that had any hope of success or even survival was a marriage of convenience.'

'I know. That's what I said.'

'I thought…when you accepted my proposal…that it was a marriage of convenience you expected…and *wanted*. But…now you tell me you love me.'

'A woman doesn't choose whether or not she falls in love, Logan.' Sara's voice came out huskily. 'I hadn't meant to tell you. It somehow…just came out. I hope it doesn't embarrass you. I know you don't feel the same way. And…well, Andy told me you were only taking a second wife because of your promise to Bethany…'

'I know Andy told you that. And it's true, I did re-assure her, when I told her I'd proposed, that I would never fall in love again—'

'Logan, you don't have to explain yourself to me—'

'Dammit, woman, will you let me finish?'

The warmth in his eyes belied the frustration in his tone. Sara nodded. And waited.

'I did set out to find me a wife. And when I met you I knew exactly the kind of woman I wanted: someone the direct opposite of the hot-tempered, argumentative Mrs Sara Wynter! But then something very odd happened. I got to liking this infuriating woman, and the more I saw of her, the more I liked her. And somewhere along the line that liking changed to love.'

Sara's heartbeats pounded her lungs with such force she could hardly draw breath. 'You fell in *love* with me?'

'You said a woman doesn't get to choose whom she falls in love with…well, my darling, neither does a man.' He looped his arms around her waist. Not loosely, as was his custom, but tightly, so she felt every hard-muscled ridge of his body. 'At least—' he grinned lop-sidedly '—not this man. This man wanted a quiet, bid-dable mouse, someone who would neither excite nor frustrate and what this man got was—'

'*Me?*'

He gave a teasing groan. 'I've been fighting it for weeks. I promised Bethany I'd marry again…and I had every intention of going through the motions. But when I heard you'd been rushed to hospital—it shook me to the very core. That was when I was forced to face the truth. I couldn't imagine life without you. I'd fallen, and fallen hard.'

'Oh, Logan...'

She raised herself on her tiptoes and kissed him. She'd meant it as a quick peck, but he had other ideas.

When finally he released her, she was breathless.

'And the reason you were so shocked when I told you I was pregnant wasn't because you didn't want the baby but—'

'But because I was afraid. You hit the nail on the head when you taunted me with, "What's *your* excuse? What are *you* afraid of?" I was afraid...well, you know what I was afraid of. Afraid I'd lose you, the way I'd lost Bethany.'

For a moment, they didn't speak, and then Sara said softly, 'Wherever Bethany is now, Logan, she's resting in peace, knowing you've kept your promise.'

'My mistake was taking the words of the promise at face value. What she *really* wanted was for me to fall in love again. Which,' he said adoringly, 'I finally did.'

Sara thought she couldn't be any happier—till Logan produced her engagement ring and slipped it on her finger.

'This time,' he growled, 'it *stays* there...for ever.'

'For ever,' she echoed...but because she liked to have the last word she added, under her breath, 'And a day!'

EPILOGUE

LOGAN squinted through the eye-piece of the brass tele-scope, and grinned.

A familiar white cabin cruiser was gaily riding the choppy waters of the Straits, and it was headed directly for his private waterfront property.

He turned and crossed to the playpen behind him, where his sixteen-month-old son was playing with col-oured blocks.

'Hey, kid—' he swung the toddler up onto his shoul-ders '— company's here. Let's get your mom.'

'Mama!' Jamie chortled, digging his chubby fingers into his father's hair and clutching tightly.

Logan strode out into the hall, dipping at the doorway, just as a series of bumping sounds came from the stairs.

'Whoa there!' he said as three-year-old Mark and four-year-old Lizzie used their jean-clad bottoms to make the descent. 'One of these days you're going to—'

'They're here, darling!'

He raised his gaze as his wife's voice came from the upstairs landing. She was wearing her flirty yellow dress, faded now from many washings, but seeing her in it always made him dizzy with desire...and she knew it! Like a lovesick teenager, he drank in every sexy curve of her eye-popping figure as she ran lightly down the stairs.

Catching up one of Mark's hands, and one of Lizzie's, she moved over to him, her turquoise eyes twinkling.

'Down, boy!' she murmured, and raised her face to his.

'Mind-reader!' he growled. But he leaned over and took what was offered. With pleasure. And lingeringly.

Till Lizzie said, 'Mommie! I want to see Andy!'

They strolled out into the breezy August afternoon.

Zach was down on the jetty, tying up the boat, and Paula was waiting there for him.

Andy was coming up the beach. She wasn't alone.

'Logan...' Sara's voice held a touch of surprise. 'Andy...she's brought a young man with her.'

'So I see!'

Sara hid a smile. He didn't sound too pleased. Andy had had a few boyfriends already, but she'd never before brought one to the island. What did it mean...?

His name was Alex Merrick. He was tall, with clear grey eyes, and wavy fair hair scraped back in a ponytail.

After all the introductions were over, Logan set Jamie down, with a pat on his diapered behind, and Sara said, 'I'll take the little ones down to meet my mother and Zach. Come with us, Alex?'

He hesitated, but only briefly, before saying, 'Sure.'

Smart boy, she thought; he realises I want to give Andy a moment alone with her father.

Scowling, Logan watched them go.

Andy walked over to him and took his hands in hers. 'You don't mind my bringing Alex, do you?' she asked.

He looked down at her. 'Of course not.'

'Sometimes,' she said quietly, her gaze steady, 'I can hardly believe I'm almost eighteen.'

She was warning him...of something. Of what, he wasn't sure. Eighteen. Where had the years gone? And where had she gone, the child with the ragged haircut, the thin boyish figure? He cleared his throat. 'So…is he special, this Alex Merrick?'

'You mean is he my Prince Charming, the one you warned me would some day sweep me up and away on his white charger? I don't know, Dad. But I like him. He's a good person.'

'I think,' he said wryly, 'I'm at last beginning to understand how you felt when I started seeing Sara.'

'Like…you're losing something?'

'Yeah, like I'm losing something.'

'I know.' She chuckled, and gave his hands a squeeze. 'It'll pass. Take my word for it.'

As she dropped his hands, he smiled and said, 'Sweetie, Sara has something to tell you. Act surprised when she—'

'Oh, my lord, she's pregnant again!' Andy's eyes shone with delight…and fun. 'Is this going to be the last?'

'The last what?' came Sara's voice from close by.

He hadn't heard the small group approach; he turned his head, and shuffled his feet guiltily.

'You've told!' Sara said in an accusing tone, but she felt her lips twitch. She'd already broken the news to Zach and Paula, who had been as thrilled as she and Logan.

'I've been asking Dad if it's going to be the last,' Andy teased.

'Don't ask me,' Logan said. 'That's one decision that's entirely out of my hands!'

'The only one!' Sara retorted. 'I think we all know who's boss around here!'

But even as everybody laughed she rejoiced in the

pride and contentment she saw in his eyes. She walked over to him, and he put an arm firmly around her.

The past was behind them, and ahead lay...who knew what?

But whatever it was they would face it together.

Who could ask for anything more?

Harlequin Romance®

Get ready to meet the world's most eligible bachelors: they're sexy, successful and, best of all, they're all yours!

BACHELOR TERRITORY

Look out for these next two books:

September 1998:
WANTED: A PERFECT WIFE (#3521)
by Barbara McMahon

November 1998:
MY GIRL (#3529)
by Lucy Gordon

There are two sides to every relationship—and now it's his turn!

Available wherever Harlequin books are sold.

HARLEQUIN®
Makes any time special ™

Look us up on-line at: http://www.romance.net

HRBT3

🔷 *Harlequin Romance*®

Invites You to A Wedding!

Whirlwind Weddings
Combines the heady romance of a whirlwind courtship with the excitement of a wedding—strong heroes, feisty heroines and marriages made not so much in heaven as in a hurry!

Some people say you can't hurry love—well, starting in August, look out for another selection of fabulous romances that prove that sometimes you can!

THE MILLION-DOLLAR MARRIAGE by Eva Rutland—
August 1998

BRIDE BY DAY by Rebecca Winters—
September 1998

READY-MADE BRIDE by Janelle Denison—
December 1998

Who says you can't hurry love?

Available wherever Harlequin books are sold.

🔷 **HARLEQUIN**®
Makes any time special ™

Look us up on-line at: http://www.romance.net

HRWW2

𝓗arlequin 𝓡omance®

Coming Next Month

#3527 THE VICAR'S DAUGHTER Betty Neels
It took a tragic accident to bring plain, sensible Margo an offer of
marriage from Professor Gijs van Kessel. It was a practical proposal,
but, as Margo was taken into the bosom of his family in Holland, she
did wonder whether he might, someday, return her love....

#3528 HER MISTLETOE HUSBAND Renee Roszel
Third book in this magical trilogy
Elissa Crosby had assumed a mothering role with her two younger
sisters for years. Stubborn and independent, she couldn't confess that
her mystery Christmas guest was not the affectionate lover they
assumed, but a man who threatened to take away everything she held
dear....

Enchanted Brides—*wanted: three dream husbands for three loving
sisters.*

#3529 BE MY GIRL! Lucy Gordon
Nick Kenton had a perfectly ordered life—until Katie Deakins came to
stay. Instead of the gawky teenager he remembered, Katie was now a
stunningly beautiful woman. Worse, she was a beautiful woman intent
on turning his life upside down!

Bachelor Territory—*there are two sides to every story...and now it's
his turn!*

#3530 WEDDING BELLS Patricia Knoll
Brittnie wished her relationship with Jared Cruz extended beyond that
of boss and employee—and involved marriage! At first Jared wasn't
interested. But then his grandfather decided to play cupid, and Jared
found himself having to think again....

Marriage Ties—*four Kelleher women bound together by family
and love.*